nancy rue

'NAMA BEACH HIGH
False Friends and
True Strangers

Youth Specialties

ZONDERVAN™

WWW.ZONDERVAN.COM

'Nama Beach High Book 2: False Friends and True Strangers
Copyright © 2003 by Youth Specialties

Youth Specialties Books, 300 South Pierce Street, El Cajon, CA 92020, are published by
Zondervan, 5300 Patterson Avenue SE, Grand Rapids, MI 49530

Library of Congress Cataloging-in-Publication Data

Rue, Nancy N.
  False friends and true strangers / by Nancy Rue.
      p. cm. -- ('Nama Beach High ; bk. 2)
Summary: Sixteen-year-old Laura Duffy learns to trust God when she
experiences a series of confusing and traumatic events, including a
mysterious secret admirer, jealous classmates, a depressed friend,
and her own eventual kidnapping.
  ISBN 0-310-25180-X (pbk.)
  [1. Conduct of life--Fiction. 2. High schools--Fiction. 3.
Schools--Fiction. 4. Interpersonal relations--Fiction. 5. Christian
life--Fiction.] I. Title.
  PZ7.R88515Fal 2004
  [Fic]--dc22
                                                                        2003015865

Unless otherwise indicated, all Scripture quotations are taken from the Holy Bible: New
International Version (North American Edition). Copyright © 1973, 1978, 1984 by
International Bible Society. Used by permission of Zondervan.

Editorial and art direction by Rick Marschall
Editing by Karyl Miller
Proofreading by Laura Gross
Editorial assistance by Ted Marschall
Cover and interior design by Proxy
Design Assistance by Sarah Jongsma
Printed in the United States of America

03 04 05 06 07 08 09 / DC / 10 9 8 7 6 5 4 3 2 1

chapterone

"You're doin' great, Duffy—you're doin' great."

I glanced over at Celeste, whose blue eyes were bulging toward the windshield as if I were about to plow into a semi.

"Is that why you're gripping the seat that way?" I said.

"KEEP YOUR EYES ON THE ROAD!"

I jerked the wheel, shooting the Volvo momentarily into the oncoming lane of traffic and lunging it back.

"Don't yell!" I yelled. "You about scared me to death!"

"Yeah? Well, you're terrifying me! I think I just wet my pants."

"I thought you said I was doing great." I could feel Celeste directing her eyes at the side of my face. "I lied," she said.

Her voice was its usual husky-hoarse, made worse by the fact that her entire neck had been, to use one of her own New York phrases, "stiff as a day-old baguette" ever since we'd pulled out of her driveway. She'd even made me turn the radio off so I could concentrate. Why did I need to concentrate? She was practically driving for me.

I made a less-than-smooth stop at the light on the corner of Highway 77 and Twenty-third Street and glanced into the rearview mirror at Joy Beth. She was gazing calmly out the window between the panels of her off-blonde hair, her big swimmer's shoulders taking up three-quarters of my tiny backseat.

"Am I doing that bad?" I said.

She gave one of her signature grunts. "Not for somebody who's driving for the first time without parents."

Joy Beth didn't usually speak in sentences that long. She saved her energy for what she considered to be more important activities.

Celeste, on the other hand, used most of hers on speaking. To her, there *weren't* too many more important activities. "Light's green," she said.

I had to concentrate on pulling into the Books-A-Million parking lot. The way kids zoomed in and out of there you practically had to have eyes in the seat of your pants to avoid a ten-car pile-up.

"Everybody and their mother is here today," Celeste said.

Joy Beth gave a half-grunt. "Too bad half of them can't read."

"They just come to schmooze," Celeste said. "There's a parking place over there."

"There's no way I can get into that!" I said.

"It's not like you've got a land yacht here. Just swing out and cut it hard. Show me what you're workin' with, Duffy."

I planted my foot on the brake, rocking all three of us forward like duck decoys. The person in the Jeep behind me leaned on the horn.

"Chill, dude," Joy Beth muttered.

Celeste's voice went into that husky-low thing that always calmed me down. "Okay, you can SO do this. pull forward while you turn your wheel to the right—you got it. Now crank it hard to the left. Crank it hard!"

I was cranking so hard I was breaking into a sweat. Power steering would have been a nice touch—but, then, I was lucky to have a car at all. It was a miracle the handles on the windows worked.

"You're good on this side. Keep crankin'."

"How am I doing in the back, Joy Beth?" I said.

"Don't worry about the back." Celeste was up on her knees craning her neck toward the red Mustang on my right. "You're clear."

I gave the wheel one more shoulder-wrenching yank, and for a second I thought the wretched grating sound I heard was my arm pulling out of the socket.

Too bad it wasn't.

"Stop!" Celeste shouted.

I did, pulling my feet and hands off of everything, so the Volvo gave a final jerk and rocked back once more against the shiny, Darth-Vader-black Chevy Silverado pick-up truck I had already grazed.

"No stinkin' way!" Celeste pulled the top half of her body out through the passenger side window, while I buried my face in my hands. When she let herself back through, she said, "Way. You did a number on his paint job."

"Paint job?" Joy Beth said. "What about his whole door? He's gonna need some serious body work."

"I can't look," I said into my palms.

"Don't," Celeste said. "Here comes the owner, and he's not happy."

"Hey, I know him," Joy Beth said.

"Do I?" I said.

"Do you know Vance Woodruff? Big jaw—big ego—big bucks?"

I shook my head.

"Well, you're about to meet him." Celeste lowered her voice to a thick whisper. "Okay, so, like, don't let him know you're scared."

Like I had a choice. My heart was pounding so hard I could *hear* it, and I was pretty sure the person who was now slamming his hand on my hood could detect it as well. I also knew he was likely to pick up on how red my already-naturally-ruddy cheeks were and on the fact that I was holding back tears. The lump in my throat was big enough to choke Godzilla.

"Whatever you do, Laura," Celeste whispered, "do *not* cry."

That was, of course, my cue to burst into tears.

But Vance Whatever-His-Name-Was obviously wasn't one to be moved by female emotions. He just jabbed a finger toward his Silverado and shouted, "You see what you just did?"

"She'd have to be blind not to," Joy Beth mumbled.

Celeste curled her fingers around my arm. "Get out of the car so he doesn't feel like he can stand over you. And if you have to cry, do it with class—no snuffing up snot."

I put my hand on my door handle and then shook my head. I could see wisps of my dark hair out of the corners of my eyes, sticking straight out as if they, too, were in shock. "I can't get out this side. I'm gonna have to climb over you."

Celeste got out and extended a hand to help me extricate myself. Before I even had one less-than-graceful foot out the door, Vance had vaulted my hood and was in my face.

"I sure hope you got insurance," he said.

"Don't go gettin' all up in her dental work. Of course she's got insurance." Celeste tossed her hair and then leaned into me. "You do have insurance, don't you?"

I nodded and pulled my jacket tighter around me until my arms were crossed. I was too numb to do much else.

The peppery freckles on Celeste's nose folded over on themselves as she wrinkled it at Vance, obviously changing tactics. "Her insurance will pay for it."

For the first time since I'd known Celeste, I was watching a boy resist her. He was looking at me out of hard cobalt eyes.

"I'm really sorry," I said. "I haven't been driving all that long—"

"Ya think?" That came from a sandy-haired kid who stepped up beside Vance, his hands rolled into his T-shirt in the front, giving us a display of his six-pack abs and the tops of his plaid boxers. He was fairer and a little goofier-looking than Vance, but other than that they could have been brothers-in-popularity. Celeste didn't have to tell me they ran the school, they just looked it. A vision of their fathers dragging my father to court flashed through my mind, and my heart plummeted.

My father. I was probably going to be grounded until I graduated—from *college*.

"It's Ethan, isn't it?" Celeste said to the sandy-haired kid.

He ignored her and turned to his buddy. "Dude, before she hit you, I was behind her and she slams on her brakes for, like, no reason. I almost plowed right into her."

"Ooh," said somebody else. "She's toast."

It was a girl this time, with a feminine version of their 'tude going on. She came up behind Vance and surveyed me as if I were an oozing zit. She looked like the cover of *Seventeen*, with shimmering dark hair and flawless skin. She had probably paid more for her eyebrow waxing than my father had for my car.

"Where did you learn to drive?" she said.

"She didn't," Ethan-of-the-Sandy-Hair said.

"Enough with the sarcasm, already," Celeste said. Her charms had been abandoned, and she was now totally New York. "Let's just exchange insurance information and get outa here. We haven't got all day."

"Packed social schedule?" Seventeen said. Her icy-blue eyes sliced through Celeste and then cut up to Vance, where they nestled in. "Didn't you just *get* that truck?"

"Yeah," Vance said. And then he swore. It was nothing I hadn't heard in the halls at Panama Beach High every day since I'd been there, but knowing it was directed at me thickened the lump in my throat to the consistency of a bagel. I could feel the *Don't you dare cry again* warning as Celeste squeezed my hand.

"Where's your insurance card, Laura?" she said out loud.

A crowd gathered in front of the store, while Vance and I exchanged insurance cards, driver's licenses, and phone numbers. I managed to drop my insurance card three times as I fumbled my wallet out of my jacket pocket and then rifled through its contents like a first-time burglar. Joy Beth muttered something about calling the police to get an accident report, but that was met with a unanimous stare-down from the entire group. It was the only thing I was grateful for. If the police had appeared on the scene, I would have cried myself into a puddle.

By the time the three of us piled back into my car, all my nerves were sparking like my entire nervous system was shorting out.

"My dad's gonna kill me!" I wailed.

My father, of course, did not kill me. He didn't even ground me. He did worse.

"If I file an accident claim with the insurance company, our coverage for you is going to spike to go out of control . You're going to have to pay for the repairs out of your own pocket."

I searched his face. His eyes, which were wide and brown like mine, gave me no indication that he was kidding.

"Plus you're going to have to pay your share of the insurance from now on."

"But—how—"

Dad gave a long sigh.

"The way everybody else does it, Laura. Get a job."

He might as well have said, "Get an arm removed."

"I don't have time for a job!" I wailed to Celeste the next morning.

The locker hall was crammed with loud kids, but the guy at the locker above mine manged to hear me. "Welcome to the real world, chick," He said..

I lowered my voice. "I've got rehearsals every afternoon. I know I've only got a chorus role, but I still have to be there." I patted my jacket pockets for stuff I might need for the day. "And I've got ten tons of homework now that I'm finally in MAPPS classes. What am I supposed to do—give up sleeping?"

With her finger, Celeste pushed a wisp of the hair I'd frantically thrown into a ponytail off my forehead. Her eyes were sympathetic. "No? Everybody else looks all rested from the three-day weekend, and you look like you've been hit by a truck."

"No, I *hit* the truck." I closed my locker door with my foot and leaned against the one now vacated by Mr. Real World. "Just when everything was working out so well—whammo—I have to go and mess it up. I wish I'd never even gotten my license."

Celeste looked horrified. "Wish you'd grow chin hair before you wish that—that's your freedom!"

"It's gone now anyway. All I'm going to get to do from now on is go to school, go to work, and study."

"What about the musical?"

I shrugged miserably. "I guess I'm gonna have to drop out. Mr. Howitch is really strict about rehearsals. My life is over!"

Joy Beth appeared beside Celeste, a thirty-pound backpack perched easily on her shoulder. "She whining again?"

"No, *still*," Celeste said. " For Pete's sake, Duffy, I'll go with you to apply for jobs. We'll find something that won't completely obliterate life as we know it."

"We?" I said.

"I'll get a job, too, same place as you." She poked Joy Beth in the backpack. "We both will."

"Huh?" Joy Beth said.

"Who can't use some walkin'-around money? Besides—" Celeste grinned. "You can take us both to work and back. Ridin' with you is exciting."

"Shut up," I said.

But I had to smile back at the two of them. There was a really good reason why they were my two best friends at 'Nama Beach High, different as they were from each other and from me.

Joy Beth talked about almost nothing but the Olympic qualifying swimming she wasn't allowed to do until she could get her diabetes under control. Celeste talked about almost nothing but guys. I talked about almost nothing but singing.

Joy Beth, with her lanky parted-in-the-middle hair and her arms as solid as hams, was the epitome of jockette. Celeste, in her radically different look every day, defined the word cute. And I, the tall string bean Midwesterner with the brown hair, brown eyes, and ruddy cheeks oozed white bread from every pore.

But our friendship had grown quickly in the few months we'd known each other. We had nothing in common except that we were members of Mrs. Isaacsen's talk group. There was a mystery to our bond—a secret I didn't try to give words to because I was afraid it might lose its magic and then I would shrivel up like the raisin I had been when I first met them. They were the best things that had happened to me since I'd moved from Missouri to Florida. Mrs. Isaacsen—the fabulous counselor who ran our group—told me not to be afraid to recognize that as God.

"Once you begin to learn the secrets of God, you can't keep them to yourself," she said to me.

Oh, I shared them, mind you. Like now I hugged Celeste and patted Joy Beth on the arm (since she wasn't much for hugging) and told them I loved them before we all split for classes. They knew I prayed; and we talked about God some (with me doing a lot of the talking), mostly about things I was sure of when it came to God. But I didn't always tell Celeste and Joy Beth about the things that happened that I couldn't explain. Those I saved for my quiet times.

Which, I realized, I hadn't really had since I'd started going to rehearsals for *Grease*. But my quiet times were the biggest reason why I needed a car. The way things were at my house—with my six-year-old sister Bonnie begging me to read Dr. Seus, my mother constantly poking her head in to ask if I wanted my room re-painted, and my father constantly hammering and power-drilling our house out of danger of being condemned—I had to actually leave the place to get anything resembling quiet.

I had found a few spots down along the Bay that gave me the space and calm I needed. And if I didn't have quiet time just to BE in The Presence I had come to know as God, something invariably got so fouled up I couldn't untangle it without practically going to a monastery.

But how am I going to have time to GO there if I have to work? I thought.

Good grief, I was even whining to myself now.

I flopped down in my seat in English. Mrs. Wren was just finishing writing the assignment on the board: *Read the first chapter of* The Great Gatsby. *Compile a complete vocabulary list and write a one-page response.*

"Can I please?" the girl next to me muttered.

I loved reading all that stuff, and even more so now that I had been transferred into MAPPS, which stood for the honors classes at 'Nama Beach. Since the beginning of second semester, I was determined to graduate with a 4.0 and get a scholarship to someplace like Stanford, and until yesterday that had seemed like a real possibility, even in chemistry. I had a great tutor in Trent Newell. I'd had a great everything, in fact: a chorus role in *Grease*, Mrs. Isaacsen's talk group , and Mrs. I. herself. She was, in fact, the other best thing that had happened to me..

So—du-uh, I thought as I pulled *The Great Gatsby* out of my backpack. *Go see her! Ya think?*

I toyed with the delicate silver key that dangled from the bracelet that Mrs. I. had given to me just a few months before. She wasn't a fairy godmother. She couldn't make things like braces and a flat chest disappear. But she could always set my head straight.

I decided to go see her—before it wobbled right off my shoulders.

chapter two

M rs. Isaacsen was with another student during lunch. Sometimes I had to remind myself that I wasn't the only person she jump-started on a regular basis. I was probably one of the few she talked to about God, though. She had to be careful about that in the public school system.

By the time I got out of rehearsal that afternoon she'd left for the day. Celeste and Joy Beth greeted me at the door of the music building, both looking like they'd just been polished up and ironed out and sprayed into place. I couldn't help staring at Joy Beth.

"What?" she said. "Nothing. I mean—you look good. Not that you don't always look good. You just look—different-good."

"Quit before she decks you, Duffy," Celeste said to me. She cocked her head and grinned. "She does clean up pretty good though, doesn't she?"

Joy Beth rolled her eyes, which, for the first time since I'd known her, were fringed in mascara. Celeste had obviously done her makeover thing on Joy Beth, tidying her hair into a French braid and zipping her into a pair of khakis and a fitted white top that revealed a waistline she usually disguised under baggy sweat-shirts. I smothered a grin as I pictured Celeste holding her down while she applied the blush and lipstick. But even though Joy Beth looked like she wanted to deck *Celeste* any minute, she was actually pulling off the feminine thing pretty well.

Celeste, of course, had gone to the edge of the extreme on herself with a navy pinstriped dressed-for-success outfit. She even had a pair of gold wire-rimmed glasses perched on her nose. Every event was a chance to put on a costume for Celeste. Only this time, I wasn't sure what the event was.

"So what's going on?" I said.

"Job hunting." Celeste jerked her head toward her Mercedes—one of the many old ones her father rescued from the junkyard. "Let's go. Joy Beth's gonna drive while I do your makeover in the back seat."

"We're going right now?" I said. "But—"

"No buts. I already told your mom you'd be late for supper when I went over to your house to pick out some clothes for you." Celeste steered me toward the Mercedes. "If you're going to be a working girl, you're going to have to can the high-school-chick look."

"I *am* a high school chick!"

She nudged me into the back seat. "Today, you are a professional woman looking for your next job."

"My first job! And I don't even know where to start. I never even thought about working—"

"That's why we're doing this right now, before you think yourself into a nervous breakdown."

I submitted to the "professionalizing" of my lips and eyes while Joy Beth navigated us through the traffic to the Panama Beach Mall. Then I let Celeste drag me into the bathroom and put me into my black pants, a camel-colored turtleneck sweater, and a fitted jacket from Celeste's own closet to replace my too-big-for-me gray hooded sweatshirt jacket that had all the convenient pockets for my assorted stuff. She yanked off my hooded sweatshirt and tossed it aside with disdain.

"You definitely have to 86 this thing," Celeste said. "You've got so much stuff in the pockets, you look like a kangaroo. Why don't you just carry a purse?"

"I do carry a purse," I said. "But this is for things I want to get to

fast, like my car keys—which I definitely DON'T need right now."
"Which is why we're going job-hunting." Celeste stood me in front
of the mirror. "You look fabulous."

I definitely looked different than I usually did. The sixteen year
old that gazed back at me from the mirror could have passed for
nineteen.

"You're a shoe-in," Celeste said.

"Where?" I said.

"The Gap."

I stared at the back of her head as she led Joy Beth and me out of
the restroom and charged down the mall like an IBM executive
headed for a board meeting. "You've never shopped at the Gap in
your life!" "Who says I have to shop there? We just want to work
there." "Why?" Joy Beth said. "I hate the Gap." "Because they're
hiring." Celeste stopped in front of the Gap's window display,
where mannequins stared vacantly out of hollow-cheeked faces.

"I bet there's babies weigh more than that," Joy Beth muttered.
She was hitching around in her outfit like a kid in a scratchy Easter
dress.

"We have to focus on being professional," Celeste said, "but not
stiff—hip but not flaky—confident but not conceited." She sized us
both up one more time and then headed for the door. "Wait!" I
said. "I don't think I can be all that stuff!" "Relax, Duffy." Celeste
held the door open for me and gave me a career-woman version of
her grin. "You already *are* all that stuff."

You couldn't have proven that by the look the girl behind the
counter gave us when Celeste told her we wanted to fill out job
applications. She did a total inventory on each of us with her eyes
and then, with a shake of her highlighted blonde hair, grudgingly
handed over three forms. I was ready to bolt.

But Celeste glanced at the girl's nametag and said, "Thank you,
Wendy."

Wendy forced a smile. Her teeth were white as Chicklets. I licked
my braces. Whatever confidence Celeste had just injected into me
was fading fast.

We all followed Wendy into a small room that was bare except for
a table, some chairs, and a microwave atop a mini refrigerator. She
told us the manager *might* want to interview us after we filled out
the applications. Then, looking as if she'd rather be shot than work
with any of us, she shut the door behind her and left us there
beneath a dry erase board on which someone had written, *Dress for
work the way our customers WISH they could look.*

"I'm not so sure about this," I said. Celeste handed me a pen. "We could all three work together and have a blast. Start writing."

Joy Beth grunted. "References. Who do I put down?"

"Mrs. I. Your swim coach. I'm putting down Laura's mom. She used to work in retail."

"She sold bras at Dillard's for about three weeks!" I said.

Celeste tapped her pen on my application form. "You have to be creative. Come on, Duffy. Have a little faith in yourself, would ya?"

Faith in myself—not so much. But at least that reminded me to pray. I thought something like, *God, please don't let me look like a moron.* And then I started filling in blanks. It wasn't too tough to surrender this whole thing. What other tools did I have in the bag BUT God?

Wendy came in and took our forms and then left again, telling us to wait until she'd talked to the manager. Celeste filled up the time by peering into the refrigerator, which made me so nervous I finally said, "Celeste, stop! You're driving me nuts!"

"I just want to see what stick women eat." She gave a sage nod as she closed the fridge door. "I was right—nothing in there but Diet Coke and Slim-Fast."

Joy Beth looked panicked. "I'm not workin' here."

"Hey—it's all of us or none of us, right?" Celeste said.

I hadn't exactly thought about it like that, but right now it was probably the only way I'd agree to being employed.

And yet, there was my accident and my insurance to pay for...

The door opened, and Joy Beth and I both jumped about a foot. Celeste remained calm, hands folded at her waist, face as innocent .

"She can do interviews now," Wendy said. She pointed to me. "You first."

"Me?" I said.

Celeste poked me.

Wendy took me to a small office where a woman, who looked a lot like Sigourney Weaver *before* the aliens got to her, stood up and put out her hand .

"I'm Yolanda," she said. "Nicetomeetyouhaveaseat."

After the five seconds it took me to figure that out, I perched on a chair and tried to look enthusiastic.

Yolanda looked at me over the top of my application and said, "You don't have any experience."

I wanted to say, *I'm sorry! I'll try to do better!* But I managed to get out, "No, ma'am, this would be my first job."

"Says here you're in the music program at Panama Beach

High. They don't take slouches there."

"It's very selective. I mean, not to brag or anything—"

"It isn't bragging to point out your strengths in a job interview." Yolanda gave me another look over the application. "Remember that next time."

My heart sank to my knees. *Next time?* That had to mean that "this time" wasn't going well.

As I tried not to let complete devastation register on my face, I realized Yolanda was now leaning back in her chair, her fingers with their fashionably squared-off nails folded under her chin as she watched me. I folded my own fingers as far down in my lap as I could, so she wouldn't be able to see how I had gnawed my nails down to nothing.

"You do have a certain sense of style," Yolanda said. "And you don't mumble like you have a mouthful of marbles. I get a lot of marble-mouths in here."

"Oh," I said—eloquently.

"You've never run a cash register."

"No—"

"How are you with computers?"

"I can't program them or anything—"

"We're not looking for Bill Gates. You just have to be able to push a few keys and count out change." She peered at me again. "You don't appear to be the type to get into trouble at school."

"No ma'am—"

"Of course, we'll call 'Nama High." She glanced down at my application. "Does this Mrs. Isaacsen know you well?"

"Very well—I mean, not because I need, like, therapy, we're just—"

Yolanda stood up. "Itwasnicetomeetyou—" Another glance at the form—"Laura. I'll notify you in the next few days. I assume you're available after school and evenings—" I sucked in a breath. "I'd prefer evenings only. After four."

"Weekends?"

"Weekends are great!"

"SuperI'llgiveyouacall."

She looked toward the door. The interview was obviously over. Almost.

Just as I put my hand on the doorknob, Yolanda said, "There's another girl with you."

"Two other girls, actually."

"I'm referring to the rather large girl. Hair in a braid."

"Joy Beth," I said.

"Uh-huh. Is she a friend of yours?"

"She's one of my best friends."

"Good—then she'll be able to take it from you.

Try to discourage her from doing an interview while I talk to—" She looked down at another application on her desk— "Celeste. Your Joy Beth just doesn't have the look we go for here, and I would hate to waste her time."

She didn't say, "And mine," but I could feel it in the air between us. I pulled my mouth from its gaping-open position and nodded stupidly.

"Thanksagain!" she said.

There was nothing to do then but open the door, only to find Wendy waiting in the hallway with Celeste. Her face fell when she saw me. My expression was obviously still one of complete dismay. The instant Wendy stepped into Yolanda's office, Celeste whispered to me, "I won't take the job if you don't get it, too. There are other stores."

I walked numbly to the little break room, where Joy Beth was pacing like it was a jail cell

"Did you get the job?" Joy Beth said.

I shrugged. "I'll know in a few days. You sure you want to work here?"

"No!" Joy Beth flopped down in one of the chairs. A about a third of the French braid had already come loose and was hanging miserably down the sides of her dismal face. "I mean, I do if ya'll are." Her Florida-cracker accent was even more countrified than usual. I was sure Yolanda wasn't looking for that particular quality in a new hire, either.

"But you'd rather be swimming," I said.

She looked at me with a definite "du-uh" in her gray eyes. "But I can't do that 'til my blood sugar stops screwing up. I'm hopin' that'll be soon—I've gone three days without havin' a reaction."

"maybe you should just concentrate on that for right now and forget about getting a job. Just because I have to get one doesn't mean you've got to be miserable, too."

"I need the money if I'm goin' to the State meet in May. My mama and daddy can't afford that—not with all my medical bills. And it's not like I'm the only kid they got."

I knew Joy Beth had a whole slew of siblings, though the two times I'd been to her family's doublewide off Route 231 I'd never been able to count them because they moved too fast.

"And my mama don't pay me to do my chores. We do

chores 'cause—we got chores to do."

"Well, yeah, but—"

I was floundering, and for a second it was a relief that the door flew open and Celeste appeared, looking like she wanted to beat somebody with one of her pumps.

" I said

"Let's blow this taco stand," she said. With us on her heels, she charged through the store, leaving the hip-hugger jeans and midriff tops swinging on their hangers. By the time we got out into the mall, I could almost see steam coming out of her ears.

"We are SO not working there," she said.

"A pile of bricks has got more intelligence than those people. I say we go get about six orders of fries and regroup."

"Yeah," Joy Beth said. and she headed off toward the food court.

I started off after her, but Celeste stopped me. With her eyes still on Joy Beth's back, she spoke without moving her lips.

"Did Witch Yolanda tell you the same thing about Joy Beth she told me?"

"That she doesn't have 'the look'?," I said between my teeth.

"We never tell her."

"Never."

Joy Beth tossed a glance over her shoulder, and Celeste grinned and hurried to catch up with her.

It's okay all the way around, I told myself, *the only person who's gonna get a job there anyway is Celeste, and it's all of us or none of us.*

At dinner that night, my father said "You started looking for a job yet?" almost before we were through saying the blessing.

"You're getting a job?" Bonnie said. My little sister was famous for responding to questions that had nothing to do with her.

"I had an interview today." I said. "They said they'd call me in the next couple of days."

"Who?"

"The Gap."

"You only applied to one place?"

"It's the best place—"

Dad put his fork down. "Don't be thinking you're a prima donna, Laura. You don't have any experience. You need to take the first job somebody will give you. This isn't like when I was job-hunting. I knew what I could do and what I was worth—and even at that I had to take a cut in pay—"

You don't have to remind any of us of that, I thought. Even after several months on his new job, he was still telling us that we were recouping the losses from a half a year of unemployment and recovering the expenses of moving here from Missouri and putting any extra money into the renovation of this house Not a day went by that I didn't hear at least a mini-lecture on how we all needed to tighten our belts and be happy with less. That was why his presenting me with the used Volvo had been such a surprise.

"So don't be picky," he was saying. "Once you've worked a couple of jobs, you'll have some leverage, but for now, go with anybody who will give you a chance."

"Scott!" Mom said. "You make it sound like she's some little waif from the ghetto."

"What's a waif?" Bonnie said, spewing out mashed potatoes with every syllable.

"All I'm saying is that she'll be lucky to get something that pays minimum wage." Dad pointed his fork at me. "That's five dollars and fifteen cents an hour. You can always work your way up from there, but you have to start someplace."

"Why does Laura gotta get a job?" Bonnie said. She had obviously already figured out that my working was going to cut into our Candy-Land playing time.

"Because she has to make money to pay for her car accident," Dad said.

I asked to be excused.

"Why do you have to start in on her at supper?" I heard Mom say as I retreated to my room. "You know it's hard enough to get her to eat when she's upset like this."

"Why is she upset?" Dad said.

Oh, brother. Man, did I need some quiet time. It was too February-chilly to go down to my bench on the Bay. I'd expected a Florida winter to be warm. I tried to lie down on my bed and close my eyes and shut out everything but God. Bonnie marched in with *Stella Luna* under her arm

"You been gone all day," she said. She slithered her way into my lap and opened *Stella* over my chemistry book.

"Okay, one time," I said.

But I'd barely gotten the first line out when Mom poked her head in.

"Phone call, Laura." Her voice was breathless.

Bonnie shook her curls. "Celeste has to wait 'til we're done."

"It isn't Celeste, Punkin'," Mom said. "This is important. I'll finish the story for you." "I want Laura!" Bonnie wailed as I untangled myself from her. "You don't do the voices good like she does!"

I picked up the phone out in the kitchen.

"Laurie—It's YolandaattheGaphowareyouthisevening?"

"Fine." I hoped that was the right answer to whatever it was she'd just asked me. "I'm offering you three nights a week, six p.m. to closing, and at least one weekend day," Yolanda said. "When can you start?"

"Start?"

"Yes. You'll be training for the first few nights, but you'll be paid of course." There was a brief silence in which I couldn't think of anything to say. "You haven't taken another job, have you?" She said it as if that would be unthinkable.

"No," I said. "What about Celeste and Joy Beth?"

There was an even briefer pause. "I already told you that Mary Beth wasn't a good fit for us, and your other friend tore up her application and dropped the pieces on my desk, so that obviously eliminates her. Is your acceptance of the job contingent on my hiring them as well?"

I could almost see her dark, Sigourney Weaver eyes pointing at me.

"Because if it is, I'm afraid I'll have to advise you to look elsewhere, though I will say it will be virtually impossible for you to all get on anywhere, unless you want to work in fast food."

I didn't. The fries I'd consumed that afternoon were already making threatening noises in my intestines.

"You do what you want," Yolanda said, "but I will tell you that the package I'm offering you is quite good for someone with absolutely no experience. I was impressed with your obvious potential, and I'm willing to start you at seven dollars an hour with a guarantee of twenty hours a week—"

I didn't even have to calculate that. With my father's voice practically shouting in my head, I said, "I can start right away."

Yolanda gave a soft chuckle. "That's what I like to hear. I think you're going to work out very well for us."

I agreed to start training the next night, which was Friday. I knew Celeste was going to freak.

But I was wrong. It was worse.

chapter three

I told Celeste as soon as I got to school. As she closed her locker door and leaned against it, I expected her to blast me. But instead her eyes were wide and sadly surprised. "I knew they were gonna give you the job," she said. "But I didn't think you'd take it. Not after what that chick said about Joy Beth."

"All she said to me was that Joy Beth didn't have the look—"

"She looked every bit as good as we did! What she meant was that Joy Beth didn't look like a clone for that LOVELY girl who sneered at you at Books-a-Million the day you plowed into that —."

"I don't look like that girl either!"

"But the Gap thinks they can turn you into her, and they're gonna try." "Then why did you drag us in there in the first place?" "Because I didn't know they were like that." She put her hand on my arm. "You didn't know either, Duf', and you're so trusting of everybody, you just think they're all as good-to-the-bone as you are."

"I'm not that good—"

"Of course you are. That's why I'm best friends with you."

Celeste shifted her bag, a safari looking affair that matched her khaki cargo pants and her Army-green vest with about sixteen pockets. I was surprised she wasn't wearing binoculars around her neck to complete the effect.

"I think of you as the kind of person that's gonna go right to the phone and call that Rolinda woman—"

"Yolanda—"

"And tell her you've come to your senses and you don't want her stinkin' job."

Her eyes were so sure of my infinite goodness, I almost asked her for fifty cents to make the call. But I had to shake my head.

"Why not?" she said.

"Because my dad—"

"He'll get it if you explain it to him."

"All he gets is that I have to pay for the reapirs on the Volvo and my insurance from now on or I don't drive."

"Then don't drive."

I could feel my eyes widening. "You're the one who said that car was my freedom! How am I supposed to get home from rehearsal in the afternoons and—"

"I'll take you wherever you wanna go. Come on, Duffy, it's the principle of the thing. This is about Joy Beth's rights as a human being."

I was glad the bell rang just then because I was about to ask, *What about MY rights?* But I don't think that would have been a good idea. She might have answered me.

As it was, she arched an eyebrow at me—an eyebrow that said, *So are you going to make that phone call?*

But we both knew I wasn't. What I did was fight my way to the counseling office through the surging crowd of kids trying to get to class before the last bell rang, and sign up for an appointment with Mrs. Isaacsen after school. Nobody else better have a crisis before then.

Nobody did. That afternoon, Mrs. I. had the teapot ready. "Is Lemon Zinger all right?" she asked.

I nodded and took a steaming cup from her. It was my usual mug—the one from the Metropolitan Opera in New York. She was always telling me I was going to get there someday. Right now, I wasn't sure I was even going to get to the Panama Beach Mall. I'd stopped singing in the shower over the last few days, and that was never a good sign. This conversation was hopefully going to help me decide about the job for good so I could get myself back. I wrapped my fingers around the Met mug and let its warmth ease into me. Between that and Mrs. I.'s Chantilly-powder smell, I was feeling calmer already and we hadn't even started talking yet.

"Those wheels are turning pretty fast in there," she said, nodding at my head. "You still reeling from your accident?"

I could feel my eyes popping. "How did you know about that?"

"Oh, honey, CNN can't deliver news as fast as these kids around here. You want to talk about it?"

I launched into the story, finishing up with that morning's conversation with Celeste. "I've been asking God what He wants me to do—you know, doing the surrender thing," I said. "And I thought my getting the job was maybe it. But if I take it, Celeste is going to hate my guts, and she's my best friend. I kind of need God to hurry up because I'm starting to feel out of control—you know, the way I used to."

Mrs. Isaacsen smiled. I loved the way she looked at me with her warm, chocolate-colored eyes and never judged me, no matter how stupid I was acting.

"You already know there is power in trusting God beyond your circumstances," she said, "beyond the no-car situation and all of that."

"I'm trying," I said. "But I think I need more."

"All right then." I could almost hear the refined Southern accent forming the words in her head as she sipped thoughtfully. "I think there are two things you can learn from this situation and only you and God can decide how that's going to play out."

"Okay," I said.

"One—God will use you wherever you are to give you more power. Just because you're all settled in now with good classes and friends and a role in the musical, that doesn't mean those are the only ways God intends to use you." She gave a little shrug of her sweater-clad shoulders. "So God just takes the next thing in your life and teaches you to have more of His power through it."

"So am I going to get more power by working at the Gap and losing my friends, or by turning down the job and keeping my friends, who I'm probably gonna lose anyway after I sponge off of them for rides—movies—"

"Why don't you let me give you the whole scenario before you talk yourself into a pit?" Mrs. Isaacsen said. Deep crinkles were radiating from her eyes, which meant she was holding back a smile. She reached over and touched the silver key on my bracelet. "The other thing to consider is what I told you when I gave you this: Once you start living the power of surrendering to Godyou have to share it."

I blinked. "And that helps how?"

"Part of making this decision will be seeing who you need to share it with."

"Celeste and Joy Beth." I said it without hesitation, but I was already seeing visions of my father's head exploding when I told him I'd decided not to take the only job offer the little waif from the ghetto was ever going to get.

" I'm sure Celeste and Joy Beth are some of the people you're supposed to share with," Mrs. Isaacsen said. "There could be others. AND you also have to figure out the best way to do that."

"I sure can't do it when they're not speaking to me!"

"But you don't know for sure that's going to happen.

I glanced at my watch. If I didn't RUN to the music wing, I was going to be late for rehearsal. As cool a teacher as Mr. Howitch was, he still expected us to act like professionals, and he cut us very little slack if we didn't.

Mr. H. was just gathering the cast together for opening notes when I got to the theatre. I dropped my backpack and joined Deidre, my fellow chorus member, on the floor in the orchestra pit. Mr. H. always used it as a place to gather.

"Duffy," Gregor, our stage manager, called out.

"Here!" I said.

"You just made it," Deirdre whispered through her tiny, bud-like lips.

Her eyes were blinking rapidly behind the lenses of her black-rimmed glasses. It seemed to me that her wild red hair was even wilder than usual. She was in fact trying to force it into a clip, which she stuck in her teeth as she took one of the papers that were being passed around and handed the stack to me. I was as serene as a monk compared to her, which partly explained why I liked her. That and the fact that she'd believed in me enough to drag me to Mr. Howitch and make me audition for him when this last-minute part had come open. Without her, I wouldn't even be in Grease.

"Oh," she said, squinting at the paper, "this is about H-Week."

"H-Week?" I said.

"H—for Hades."

"All right, folks, listen up."

Mr. Howitch was perched on the top step of the carpeted stairs that led up to the stage. He always reminded me of a funny little bird with a mustache when he sat like that.

"What you have in your hands," he was saying, "is a schedule for our final week of rehearsals, which is coming up. You'll notice that this indicates a change in our normal rehearsal routine."

I had already noticed that, and I was getting a sick feeling somewhere in my esophagus. We had no afternoon practices during H-Week—it was all evening rehearsals. I stifled a groan.

And then I made a decision: I wasn't taking that job. I didn't care if I didn't have a car ever in my whole life. Getting into this show had been a total God-thing. Nobody just walked in from another school and snagged a part in one of Mr. Howitch's famous musicals—and I had. Music was everything. I couldn't jeopardize it.

I was already planning my speech to my father, in which I would tell him that he could sell the Volvo, when Gregor called out, "Places for act two." I jumped and hurried to the section on stage left, which was marked off for the soon-to-arrive set.

Gregor was an exchange student from Germany whose accent was too thick for him to have a speaking part and, besides, he seemed to enjoy the power he could wield as stage manager.

"Nata-LIE!" Gregor shouted at a girl who was just about to go out the auditorium door. "Where you are going?"

You'd have sworn he was the Gestapo.

But Natalie whipped around and glared at him. She had sandy-blonde hair styled in one of those weed-whacker cuts. There was just something about her phoniness that seemed to type-cast her for playing the role of Patty. Although at the moment she made me think of a rabid beaver.

"I'm going to the freakin' bathroom!" she said.

I froze and watched Gregor. The teeth obviously didn't scare him a bit.

"You should take care of zeez sings before the rehearsal," he said. "Places." And then he stared her down, one arm pointing to the stage, until she let go of the door and marched up the side steps to her place.

All the way across the stage, I could hear her muttering, "Fine. But if I pee on the floor, you're the one who's going to wipe it up."

I looked nervously at Mr. Howitch, but he evidently hadn't heard it because he plunged right into act two, and I did, too. Within five minutes I had forgotten about Natalie, Gregor, the job I was going to turn down, and the car I was going to give up. It might have only been a chorus role, but I gave it my all. By the break, I was on a high.

Everybody scurried for the soda machines and the restrooms, although, for someone who had supposedly been desperate to relieve herself for the past hour, Natalie sure didn't make a fast break for the toilet.

I was headed for the water fountain, empty water bottle in hand, when somebody said, "Hey, Laura D. How's it going?"

I looked around and saw K.J. O'Toole, one of the girls in Mrs. Isaacsen's group. It was jarring to see her outside Mrs. I.'s office.

K.J. and I definitely didn't travel in the same circles. "What are you doing here?" I said. I knew she'd been dropped from the fall play because she'd been suspended for talking back to a teacher.

She walked over to me, a gob of silver chains bouncing off the side of her hip. Even in the semi-darkness of backstage, I could see that her pants were skin tight, as was her T-shirt. How she got away with some of her outfits under the 'Nama High dress code, I could never figure out.

She tilted her chin up at me, bouncing the three-inch-long beaded earrings.

"I'm on stage crew," she said. "I'm on probation with Howitch, but he likes me. As long as I don't get in trouble anyplace else, he'll keep me on."

"You like being a techie?" I said. She shrugged, "It's okay. I'd rather be acting—but I can't sing for squat so this show was out for me. I'm working on my audition for the spring play, though. *The Glass Menagerie*."

"Really?" I said. "We read that in English class."

"Cool play. There are only two parts for women, though. There are so many good people in the department, I'll probably have to kill somebody to get the part."

Although about half the time she looked at people like she was thinking, *You want a piece of me?* I didn't think she'd go as far as murder. She had a huge desire to see that justice was done, which was what got her into trouble. When Gregor called places again, I silently hoped she'd get through this production without getting suspended again.

I was wiped out when rehearsal was over, and I headed for Mom's van in the student parking lot. I'd been surprised that morning when she told me to take it instead of riding the bus, and I made a promise to myself to thank her big time when I got home.

I was so tired I wasn't sure I could have handled running for the late bus right now.

It was a good kind of tired, though, and I still turned on the CD player and belted it out with Martina McBride. I had always loved just about every kind of music but rap and country western, but since I'd moved to Panama Beach I'd gained a new appreciation for country music.

I drove about ten miles per hour over the speed limit getting home. I really needed to go over this whole thing with Celeste. I glanced at the clock on Mom's dash. If I skipped dinner, I could squeeze in a phone call to her. I could also skip changing my clothes I didn't have to have "the look" to turn down a job.

Celeste's phone number was already in my head when I pulled into our driveway, but it went out like everything else as I slammed on the brakes and stared.

There was my Volvo, all fixed and polished and parked like it was on display in a show room. *Yikes, did Dad read my mind?* I thought. *Did he already know I wasn't going to take the job and he's got it ready for sale?*

I had a heavy sense of foreboding as I collected my backpack and dragged myself into the house. Everybody was already starting to eat, but nobody scowled at me for being late. In fact, Dad was grinning his face off. My stomach started to knot.

"Did you see your car?" he asked.

"Yes," I said. "Why did you fix it up?"

"Aren't you pleased?" Mom said. "Doesn't it look great?"

She was bobbing her head up and down at me as if she were giving me a giant clue.

"But I thought I had to pay to have it fixed," I said.

"You do," Dad said. "But since you went right out and got yourself a job, I had your car fixed so you could drive it to work. You can just pay me out of your earnings. Shouldn't take more than a paycheck or two at seven dollars an hour."

My father actually looked proud. Mom was beaming as if I'd just decided I wanted to learn how to crochet. Now there was no way I could tell them I'd decided not to take the job. Not only were they thinking I was the poster girl for responsibility—but Dad had already paid for the damages. How else was I going to pay him back?

Sell the car! I wanted to say. *I don't care about it!*

But they obviously did. And if I were going to remain their beloved, mature, dependable image of a daughter, I had to care, too.

I summoned up the enthusiasm to say, "Thanks, Dad. I guess I'd better get to work."

I refused my mother's offer to pack me something to eat on the way to the mall, then hurriedly jumped in and out of the shower, French-braided my hair, and put on something resembling Gap-Girl. When I got inside the Volvo and smelled the brown bag full of Mom's ham and fresh biscuits sitting on the passenger seat, I wanted to throw up. Being in that car felt suddenly suffocating. I didn't even turn on the radio.

All right, Laura, I told myself as I managed to get up Route 77, *this isn't where you want your head to be the first night on the job.*

By the time I parked the car, I was shaking like a leaf. I closed my eyes.

"God?" I whispered. "I'm just trying to surrender here. So – please – use it."

Then I just sat there and listened, hoping God would whisper back

But there was no whisper. Wishing to be struck by some kind of paralyzing disease, I got out of the car.

chapterfour

W endy greeted me wth a curled lip. As I followed her to the
back of the store, I asked myself why people like Wendy
were all such attractive people when they were talking to each
other—and such twisted folk when they turned on the rest of us.

Wendy told me to go into the manager's office. Yolanda didn't
look up when I went in, even as she said,
"WelcometotheGapTeam," and handed me a nametag. It bore the
title: LAURIE, TRAINEE.

"It's Laura," I said—feebly—as she picked up a handful of papers
and led me across the hall to the break room.

"What?" she said. She was busy dumping two abandoned Diet
Coke cans into the trash with her fingers extended, apparently to
avoid contamination.

"It's Laur-UH—not Laur-EE."

Yolanda finally glanced up and her eyes flickered across my
nametag.

"Oh," she said. "Well—leave it for now. You'll get a new one when you're done training, and I don't think it's going to take you as long to finish as it does most people." She gave the trash can another disdainful look. "You strike me as a cut above the usual."

When she sailed out, I filled out the wad of forms she gave me, most of which were about taxes. That broke me out into a cold sweat. What did I know about taxes?

I fumbled my way through and tried not to look completely clueless as I emerged from the break room and went toward Yolanda's office door.

"Over here," she called to me from the direction of the store floor. She was snapping her fingers at me, probably because once again my name had apparently escaped her. I followed the call like an obedient dog.

"Wendy is going to train you," Yolanda said, still without looking at me but letting her dark beady eyes scan the place like a surveillance camera. "She'll show you everything but the dressing room drill, which is a bit more involved because of the shoplifting issue—Wendy—" Yolanda snapped her fingers at Wendy, too, although she was less obedient than I had been and took her time getting to us.

"She's all yours," Yolanda said, her gaze still roaming.

Wendy looked less than thrilled. She was Gap Girl. I was not. I might as well have outfitted myself at the Goodwill, the way she was looking at me.

"Come on," she said with a sigh. "I guess you should just follow me around and watch what I do. It's not rocket science."

Wonderful. She was the pedigreed poodle. I was the mutt.

There weren't that many customers at first, and Wendy stealthily avoided the ones that were there.

"Why do old women come in here?" Wendy muttered to me as we watched one of the other sales girls greet a forty-year-old with a figure like Helen Hunt. "There's nothing in here that works for them."

For the most part, we stocked some shelves and tidied up some others, although Wendy usually just folded the top items and wadded up the others underneath. When clerks from the dressing rooms called for different sizes on things, we went for them, which at least gave me a chance to learn where things were.

"If you want to stay on Yolanda's good side," Wendy said to me in a rare moment of niceness, "always look busy."

Around seven, business started to pick up. The place suddenly looked like the halls at 'Nama High. At that point, Wendy out maneuvered the other sales people to get to customers she obviously knew. Most of them resembled her: beautiful, perfect, and rich.

"How are you finding everything?" she'd coo.

Most of them laughed or rolled their eyes like they were in on her attempts to stay on Yolanda's good side. Then she'd lead them off to the new merchandise or the stuff that was on sale and leave me to trot along behind.

When they went to the dressing room to try things on, she and I would loiter outside and try to "look busy."

Just about all of Wendy's friends bought something. She—and I—carried the items up to the counters, where two experienced Gap employees manned the cash registers.

"Is that all they do?" I said.

"What?" Wendy said. She squinted her eyes as if I were getting on her last nerve, when in fact it was about the first question I'd asked all evening.

"Those cashiers. Do they just—"

"On busy shifts you have one job—you're either dressing room, front counter, or floor." She huffed at me. "We're obviously floor shift tonight."

"So—do I need to learn to run the cash register?"

"Yes." She rolled her eyes. "Owen teaches that, but he's not here tonight. And you don't need it tonight anyway, so—"

She looked extremely hopeful that I was going to get it soon because she was obviously tired of trying to penetrate my thick skull. I nodded and knew my face wasn't as red as it felt.

There was a slight lull in the action at one point, and since none of Wendy's pals were currently on the floor, she announced she was going to "take a pee." I went with her.

"I never knew so many kids shopped on Friday nights," I said as I needlessly washed my hands while she "peed."

"The good house parties don't start until later, like when we're closing. So what else is there to do?" she said .

But as Wendy half-heartedly passed her hands under the faucet, she looked at me in the mirror and almost smiled.

"So where do you live?"

"In the Cove."

"Oh. Who do you party with?"

"Excuse me?" I said.

"On the weekends. Who do you party with?"

"I hang out," I said, carefully picking my way through, "with Celeste Mancini—" "She's the girl you were in here with the other day." "Yeah—she's my best friend. Her and—" "The jock." Wendy dismissed Joy Beth by turning toward the door, while I glared at her back. I still nearly ran into her when she stopped short and looked at me over her shoulder.

"The only reason I work here is so I'll know when all the new stuff comes in and I can tell my friends," she said. "I don't really need the money."

"Really," I said.

When it was time for our break, several of Wendy's friends came back to sweep her off to the food court. I wasn't invited to go along, not that I would have gone. But I didn't know what to do instead, so I went back to one of the displays we'd been straightening up earlier that had hidden messes underneath. Not having Wendy sneering at me or showing me how to get away with doing practically nothing was a relief. For the first time all night, my shoulder blades relaxed. They sprang back to attention when somebody said, "What are YOU doing?"

I looked up to see Yolanda with her lips pulled into a pinch.

"I'm—straightening—"

"Didn't you two already do this?"

Okay—what to do now? Tell Yolanda that Wendy is a slacker, or look like one myself?

"Don't try to "get by" just doing busy work, Laurie. Go practice on some customers." "Yes, ma'am—" "Where's Wendy?" "On break." "What about you?" "I—" "You can't cut out early just because you don't take a break." "I wasn't—" My voice trailed off as Yolanda suddenly went into a squat in front of the display and yanked out the sleeve of a sweater I hadn't gotten to yet. "Didn't Wendy show you how we do things around here?" she said. She showed me how SHE does things, I wanted to say.

"Every piece of merchandise is folded like the ones on top." She stood up and snapped her fingers at the guilty pile. "Redo this whole thing. Is there something I can help you ladies with this evening?"

It took me a second to realize that she was now talking—in a smooth, butter-melting voice—to a customer with a mortified-looking twelve-year-old boy shifting behind her. She wafted them off to jeans while I went back to trying not to gnash my teeth and hate Wendy. The worst part was that I wasn't going to be able to vent about all of this to Celeste because she'd just say she'd TOLD me so.

I somehow got through the rest of the shift without either making a complete fool of myself or running into Yolanda again. That is, until nine, when I was clocking out in the break room.

"How'sitgoing?" she said as she perused the timecards.

"Fine," I said.

She held the door open for me and followed me back out onto the floor. "I was watching. You really didn't do badly for your first night. One little folding glitch—not a huge deal."

"I learned from that," I said. *Never work with Wendy again.*

"Love it," she said. She was already walking away from me when she added, "I wish I had about six more with your attitude."

The minute she disappeared I could feel eyes on me. I turned around to see not only Wendy, but also Seventeen Girl from my accident scene, Natalie from *Grease* rehearsals, and another "chick"—as Celeste would have dubbed her— from my American history class. I'd watched her breeze into second period every day looking poised and pulled-together. She was sort of Hispanic look-ing, though her skin was the color of chocolate milk—heavy on the milk—and her bouncy, shoulder-length hair was light brown with blonde highlighted stripes. She was one of those girls who wasn't inherently drop-dead gorgeous, but who seemed to know what to do with her best features. I had actually kind of admired that about her.

As soon as I looked at them, they all seemed to be staring right through me at something beyond us in the store. I even turned around to see what it was. When I turned back toward them, they had closed in on themselves. I gave them a wide berth as I headed for the door, but I couldn't help overhearing what they were saying.

"That top is SO cute, Wen'," Hispanic Girl said.

What was her name? I'd heard Mr. Beecher say it at least twenty times. It was a boy's name, I was pretty sure. Joey? Frankie? No—

"You look fabulous in it," Seventeen Girl said.

Natalie gave a snort-sniff-snuff sound. "It'd look fabulous on me. Take it off and give it to me, Wendy."

"Real nice, Nats!" Boy-Name said.

"Shut up!" "Nats" said. And I'd complained about being called "Laurie."

"Shhhh! You're gonna get me in trouble."

I sneaked a peek to see Wendy standing on tiptoes to survey the store. I found myself looking around for Yolanda, too.

"Sorry," said Boy-Name.

"So what time do you get out of here?" Seventeen Girl said. "Stevie says there's a party—"

Stevie! Only, Mr. Beecher always called out "Stephanie" during roll.

The group began to break up.

"Can't you get somebody else to close for you?" Seventeen Girl was saying.

"Right, Gigi—like I'm gonna ask the new girl to close for me."

They all looked directly at me.

"Uh, hello, rude-to-her," Stevie said to Wendy. She squinted her dark eyes at my nametag. "Sorry, Laurie. I doubt you want to be called 'the new girl'."

Then she bounced her hair back to Wendy—and Gigi—and Natalie—and lowered her voice to a whisper. Now that I actually had a name, I obviously couldn't be trusted with party information.

Like I'm so gonna crash it, I thought.

I dragged myself to the car. I had to turn the radio up full blast so my eyelids wouldn't slam shut on the drive home.

The over-the-stove light was on in the kitchen when I got there, casting a ghostly glow on the plate of oatmeal cookies and the note Mom had left me.

I promised Bonnie you would come in and say good-night to her when you got home, she'd written at the bottom. Next to it was a tiny smiley face. We both knew Bonnie would be dead to the world and drooling by this time. But I still crept into her room. Strawberry blonde curls tumbled over her forehead, and her cheeks were so relaxed and so flushed with sleep, she looked like she was three years old again.

I squatted down to retrieve the covers Bonnie had kicked onto the floor. As I pulled them up around the shoulders of her pink Barbie 'jammies, something thudded softly to the floor. It was *Stella Luna*, and it opened expectantly to the first page as if Bonnie had instructed it to, should I EVER finally come home. I felt like crying as I stumbled to my own room and fell into bed with my wrong nametag still pinned on.

* * * * * *

I woke up the next morning and heard a ringing sound that wasn't my alarm clock. I lay there in bed, digging the nametag's pin out of my chest and waiting for somebody to answer the phone. When I heard a long beep give way to Celeste's New York accent, I tore off the covers and stumbled toward the kitchen and the sound of her husky voice saying, "Hi, how ya doin', Duffies—"

I snatched up the receiver. "Hi!" I said breathlessly.

"Oh! You're there."

"Sorry. I guess everybody else is still asleep."

"At eleven a.m.? YOUR little sister?"

"No way it's that late!"

Celeste chuckled. "What—did you have a hot date last night? That why you didn't answer my e-mail?"

"No," I said carefully. "I had to work."

The chuckle went stiff.

I perched on a stool at the snack bar and tucked my bare feet up into my pants, which were by now a mass of slept-in wrinkles.

"I was going to quit," I said. "I really was—but then my dad—"

"You can tell me about that later. I've gotta leave in like, ten minutes, and I won't be back 'til late Sunday night—"

When we hung up, I thought, *Wow. Just—God—wow.*

My second day at work went better than my first night, actually. Wendy wasn't on that shift, and none of the Gap Girls came in. I even waited on some customers without supervision, which seemed to impress the sales quota right out of Yolanda because she told Owen, the guy I was working with, that the rest of them were going to have to start hustling if they wanted to keep up with me.

As she walked away, Owen glared at her from beneath his eyebrows and fiddled with his earring.

"Like I don't already bust my tail for the Gap," he said, barely moving his lips.

"I don't think I'm that good or anything," I said quickly.

"She does, and that's all that counts." Owen tilted his head almost to his shoulder as he looked at me like he was ready to disclose essential information. I found myself tilting my own head to match it.

"She's always talking about this 'team' we're supposed to be," Owen went on. His eyes rolled almost up into his head. "It's not a team; it's a private club—and you can only belong to it if she likes you."

"So—what happens if she likes you?" I said.

Owen gave a shrug and wagged his head to the other side. "You got me. I'm not in the club."

I wasn't sure I wanted to be either. But I had a feeling it wasn't good if Yolanda didn't like you and you had a debt to repay and insurance premiums to meet—

NO, I told myself firmly. *I'm going to pay Dad back, and then I'm going to tell him to sell the car. And then I'm going to quit.*

There was no God-whisper, but it was the best thought I'd had in a while.

It was after ten again when I finally left, and a pile of homework the size of Mount Rushmore waited for me on my desk at home. It was 1:30 a.m. before I tumbled into bed. I could barely drag myself out of it when the alarm went off at six.

I prayed all the way to school that I'd be able to keep my eyes open at least until I got there. But they sprang wide open when Celeste started opening my car door before I came to a complete stop in the parking space.

"Hey, your car's fixed!"

I set the brake and hauled out my backpack. "Good morning, Celeste. Nice to see you, too. My weekend was fine thank you. And yours?"

"Sorry." Celeste pressed her hand to her forehead.

"I was up half the night doing homework. This job is already killing me."

"So quit."

I sighed as I squatted down in front of my locker.

"I can't quit yet—not until I pay back my dad. He had my car fixerd and now ——"

I stopped short as I pulled my locker door open and a box tumbled out and onto my foot. With an "Ouch!" they could have heard in the freshman locker hall on the other side of campus, I picked it up. It was a wooden box—heavy—shaped like a treasure chest, complete with brass hinges and an ancient looking padlock.

"Duffy, if you're going to keep your ill-gotten booty in your locker, you need to cram it in there a little better," Celeste said above me. "You could break a toe with that thing. What the heck is it, anyway?"

I had no idea what it was, but as an envelope slid out of the locker behind it, I could guess where it had come from. I slid the note inside the pocket of my backpack before Celeste could see it.

I didn't feel like discussing the Secret Admirer with her right now.

And that had to be who it was from. I hadn't heard from him—her—whoever—since before Christmas, but there was no mistaking the S.A.'s MO: a mysterious gift accompanied by an off-white parchment envelope with my name written in perfect calligraphy across the front.

Perhaps "mysterious" wasn't a strong enough word. Maybe "bizarre" was better. The mega-vine the S.A. had left me last fall had everybody thinking I was some kind of gardening freak. There was no telling what was in Captain Hook's chest.

When Ms. Wren set us to work dissecting chapter three of *The Great Gatsby*, I put Daisy and Gatsby off for the moment and opened the envelope. I pulled out the note slowly, reverently, and imagined fingers—someone's fingers—precisely matching up the corners of the parchment and pressing the fold into place with one smooth, perfect glide of the fingertips. My own fingers were already moist with little sparkles of sweat as I eased it open. The expected pristine strokes of ink awaited me.

> *Fill this with priceless treasures. I know you can.*
> *Your Secret Admirer.*

As always, the S.A.'s words found their way into my chest, where they created an elusive far-away warmth. But this time, there was a wisp of disappointment, too. I didn't feel encouraged or inspired— heck, I didn't even feel admired. Instead, I felt another expectation add its weight to the load I was already hauling around.

Priceless treasures? I thought as I tucked the note back into its envelope and turned back to F. Scott Fitzgerald. *Honey, every dime I make is going into my father's coffers.*

I decided it was a good thing our group was meeting with Mrs. Isaacsen during activity period that day. Maybe I could set up a time to talk to her alone later. Maybe if I begged, she'd give me some clearer answers.

chapter five

M rs. Isaacsen was passing around a plate of cookies when I got to her office. She also tossed each of us a can of our favorite soda—with a warning not to let them fizz all over her multi-colored rug.

"What's the occasion?" Celeste said.

"Cure for the mid-winter doldrums," Mrs. Isaacsen said. "I'm so sick of gray weather, I needed a lift. I thought ya'll might, too." She was passing out envelopes to each of us.

"What's this for?" K.J. said.

Over in her usual corner, Michelle Martine said, "You'll probably find out if you'll just wait."

She ran the tips of her fingers against the African-American-black hair she had smoothed into a bun, her full, serious mouth pulled into a line. I'd decided a while back that since Michelle looked like she could handle the responsibilities of a thirty year old, she must feel like one, too. But who could know for sure? She was even more closed-up about her feelings than Joy Beth when we were in our group, and I never saw her any other time.

"So—can we open them?" Celeste said.

"I already did. Thanks, Mrs. I.," K.J. said. It was a rare moment of respect for authority.

Joy Beth transferred an unopened caffeine-free Diet Pepsi from one hand to the other and back again. *Okay, I thought, she really IS mad at me. She won't teven look at me.*

Celeste gave her a nudge. "Open your card.."

"I would actually prefer that you all open them sometime when you have a quiet moment alone," Mrs. I. said.

Like I have so much of that right now, I thought as I tucked mine into my backpack. I felt a wave of sadness, as if I were homesick.

"For now," Mrs. Isaacsen was saying as she picked up her frog mug, "why don't you sit back and let's ponder a new question: What is your most pressing personal concern at this point in your life?"

Celeste gurgled. "That's easy! "

"I didn't ask you to name something you don't think you could live without. I'm talking about something deeply impor- tant— defining."

"Examples?" K.J. said.

Mrs. Isaacsen started ticking off fingers. "Educational achieve- ment. The ability to handle life's challenges. Relationships—" She slanted a twinkly-eyed glance at Celeste—"solid relationships. Personal performance. What the future holds. Spiritual, moral, or ethical issues. Enjoyment—pleasure. But your choices aren't limited to those."

"What else is there?" Celeste said, grinning.

"Do we have to pick just one?" I said. "I think I have ALL those problems."

"Don't think of them as problems. Look at them as—well, this will work for you, Laura: Look at them as keys to the future you want. Which one do you want to hold in your hand right now?"

The one on my bracelet should be all I need, right, God? I thought. *It has been for a couple months now.*

So why wasn't just surrendering to God working anymore?

I toyed absently with the charm. And then it was as if it accepted its mission and opened a lock in my brain: *Well, du-uh. Finding the next KEY is the key.*

That meant I really needed to talk to Mrs. I. alone—soon.

"Are you gonna make all of us share ours?" K.J. said.

Mrs. Isaacsen lightly smacked her own forehead with the heel of her hand. "Dang it, I left the instruments of torture at home." She gave K.J. a half frown. "Now, since when have I ever 'made' you tell anything?"

"True," K.J. said.

"I can tell mine!"

All of us, except Joy Beth, looked at Celeste, who was peeling off her glaring-green satin P.B. Stockcar Association jacket like she was really warming up to the topic.

"Can I guess hers?" K.J. said.

"You know the answer to that," Mrs. Isaacsen said. "Goahead, Celeste."

"Don't everybody go fainting or anything, but mine isn't boys. It's priorities. And not mine—somebody else's."

"The key to a satisfying future for you is somebody else'spriorities?" K.J. said.

"That isn't so unbelievable."

I stared at Michelle after she said that. She never broke the put-it-in-the-form-of-a-question rule—or probably any rule, for that matter.

"Do you want to talk about that, Michelle?" Mrs. Isaacsen said.

"No," Michelle said.

I could tell by the way K.J. was bobbing in her seat that she was dying to push for details, but the one thing we all knew about Michelle—probably the only thing—was that when she was done talking, she was done talking. She was obviously done now.

"It isn't my whole future," Celeste continued. "But I'm having trouble being happy right now because another person is making some bad choices."

"What's his name?" K.J. said, and then slapped her hand over her mouth.

I already knew it wasn't a "him." It was a her, and the her was me. Although Celeste wouldn't look at me, I glared at the side of her face.

When the meeting was over, Joy Beth asked Mrs. I if she could hang with her for a few minutes. I took off after Celeste.

"What is the DEAL?" I said. "I TOLD you why I have to keep the job."

"Whatever," Celeste said. She stopped outside the entrance to the courtyard where we always ate lunch. "And what's going on with Joy Beth? How come she wants to talk to Mrs. I instead of us?"

I peered closely at Celeste. The tears I was hearing in her voice matched the ones shimmering in her eyes.

"This is really tearing you apart," I said.

"You don't even know. Look, Duff, I never had girlfriends before. It was always guys 'til you and her. Thinkin' about losin' one of you is freakin' me out here."

"She's not gonna die," I said.

"But she might just dump us. She's already going to Mrs. Isaacsen with her stuff. It's not like when some guy ditches you. There's always plenty more where he came from, y'know?"

I didn't, but I nodded anyway.

"But if she breaks off from us, there isn't another Joy Beth Barnes—there's only one, just like there's only one Laura Duffy. You just don't go replacin' girlfriends. Good ones are too hard to find."

Her voice was cutting in and out like a bad cell phone connection. "I just need you, Duffy—and her. I can't be losin' you two, all right?"

I couldn't talk, so I just shook my head.

We both worked on not crying for a couple of minutes, and then she sat up straight on the concrete bench we were sharing in the courtyard, our backs to the rest of the high school world.

"Let's go by her house after you get out of rehearsal," she said, "and just camp out there until she talks to us."

My heart took a nosedive. "I can't. I have to work."

She didn't say anything. She didn't have to. Her shrug said it all.

"I'm only working there 'til I get my dad paid off," I said. "He fixed my car without me knowing and now I have to give the money back to him. Don't you see? It's like I'm in a trap."

Her mouth softened into a wobbly line.

"I hear that," she said. "I don't know what I'm gonna do about my dad. He thinks I'm gonna work in his pit crew for the rest of my life. I even feel like I have to wear this stupid jacket he bought me this weekend." She shook her head, ponytail bouncing through the opening in the back of the matching Stockcar Association ball cap. "Just get him paid off soon as you can, okay, Duffy?"

* * * * * *

I was tired when I got to work that night. I'd even had trouble staying awake in music theory that afternoon—and that was my favorite class. I hoped Mr. Howitch hadn't noticed. Rehearsal picked me up because we were learning a dance for the finale, but the minute it was over my buns started to drag. I had to force myself to do some homework before I left for work, or I knew I'd be up half the night again.

When I went into the break room to clock in for my shift, Owen was in there, bent over textbook and pencil at the table. It looked like he was doing geometry.

"Don't say it," he said. "I know I'm a geek—you don't need to rub it in."

"Like I could," I said. "I'm a geek, too."

"You're not a geek," he said. "You are on the college track."

"How'd you know that?"

"Because a girl like you wouldn't be working here unless you had to save for college."

"You're not?"

Owen shook his head, which tonight was maroon and slicked back like parakeet feathers.

"I'm already IN college, but I'll be lucky if I make it through," he said. "I got to, though. I don't want to be working in the Gap for the rest of my life." "It doesn't seem that bad so far," I said.

Owen widened his eyes, which, for the first time, I noticed were a gentle blue, surrounded by thick black lashes. "Yeah, well, just watch your back.."

"Because...?" I said.

"Because you don't want to get involved in what goes on around here." "So, what goes on?" I said. "You don't want to know." I laughed out loud. "But you just said to watch my back!" "Just keep your eyes open so you know when to look the other way." "What?" "Because if you actually see it, you have to report it—and then— your life is over." "No stinkin' way. My life is not 'over' if I lose this job. I'll owe my father money for the rest of my life, but—"

"You don't understand." Owen shoved the textbook out of the way so he could get more in my face. "It's Them. They will make your life so miserable you'll wish it was over." "Who? Who's 'Them'?" There was a tap on the door, and Yolanda poked her head in.

"You going to cut it down to the last thirty seconds, Owen?" she said. Then she looked at me. "Don't let the rest of them be a bad influence on you."

The door closed and I scrambled to my feet.

"Just one thing, Laurie," Owen said.

"Laur-UH."

"Just remember this: I am not one of Them."

"Okay," I said and followed him out onto the floor feeling as clueless as ever.

Wendy was just flying in the front door as Owen and I came out. Natalie and Gigi streamed in behind her and stopped at the rack of microscopic stretch-knit skirts that had appeared since the night before.

"Are you finding everything you need?" I said—in my best Gap Team voice.

Gigi gave me a tepid smile. "We won't be here that long."

"If I can help you with anything, just let me know," I said.

Natalie looked at me as if I were selling poisoned Girl Scout cookies. "Wendy's our regular sales person," she said.

"Oh," I said. "Well, that's cool."

"We think so." This time Gigi didn't smile. Her look told me I was dismissed.

I hurried back to the counter to find Owen watching me—probably assessing the redness quotient in my cheeks.

"Don't waste your time on them," he murmured into my ear as he steered me toward a pile of T-shirts somebody had obviously rifled through. "They'll only deal with Wendy. But if Yolanda's watching, go ahead and ask them if they need help anyway, just so you don't get her on your back."

I picked up a T-shirt and started folding it as if Yolanda were training her sights on me at that very moment.

"Is Yolanda one of Them—whoever *They* are?"

"No. The only reason I don't respect her is because she hasn't figured out what's going on right under her nose."

Owen took off to greet a customer.

Wendy appeared from the direction of the break room, looking pale and smelling vaguely of vomit.

"I just hurled in the bathroom," she said.

Ya think? I thought. But I said, "I'm sorry."

"I think I have a fever." Wendy looked into my eyes, her own pleading. "Will you tell Yolanda I had to go home because I'm so sick?"

"Shouldn't you tell her?" I asked.

"Well, I would, but she's on the phone." Wendy put a lightly tanned hand to her mouth. "Oh, Lord—I think I'm gon' puke again. Would you—"

"Yeah, sure," I said.

She nodded—gratefully—and then instead of bolting for the bathroom, she headed for the front door. I noticed she already had her purse swinging from her shoulder. Gigi and Natalie were waiting for her, and Gigi put her arm around Wendy's shoulder and looked back at me, mouthing a "thank you" in my direction. Natalie just marched to the door and led the way triumphantly out into the mall.

I had the sinking feeling I had just made a huge mistake.

I walked in the direction of Yolanda's office with my heart pounding. Owen was suddenly at my side, carrying an armful of jeans.

"Where to?"

"I have to go tell Yolanda that Wendy had to leave because she's sick."

"Sick in the *head*! You told her you'd do that for her?"

"Ye–ah," I said slowly.

Owen put his hand on my shoulder to stop me. "She should've waited. Nobody checks out without talking to the manager in charge of the shift—and nobody agrees to do it for them or they're in just as much trouble."

"I didn't know!"

"Don't worry about it. I'll tell Yolanda ."

He dumped the pile of jeans into my arms and started off, but I grabbed him by the sleeve of his Gap shirt.

"I told Wendy I'd do it," I said, "so I really should."

"I'm already on Yolanda's list. She wants to fire me because of my hair, but she can't, and that ticks her off. I got nothing to lose—and you do." He cocked his mahogany head. "We've got to get you to college." Then he took off.

I turned to put the jeans back on the rack and I suddenly felt lonely, even in a store that was fast filling up with kids who didn't seem to have anything else to do on a Monday night except buy stuff they didn't need. I was starting to dislike them all.

At least we were so busy that my shift didn't drag. Having Wendy gone made a huge difference, and I didn't even take my thirty-minute break at 8:30, even though Owen tried to make me.

"If that little broad hadn't faked being sick, we could take our break together," he said. "Then you'd have to go."

"She did throw up," I said. "I could smell it on her breath."

"Of course she threw up." Owen pretended to stick his finger down his throat.

"No stinkin' way!"

"They've had a lot of practice."

"You mean, they're like, bulimic?"

"Did I say that?"

Owen blinked innocently at me and then said, "At least go have a Coke. Matter of fact, go have a seven-course meal. You look like you could use it."

I couldn't have eaten if I'd tried. I was having a little trouble not throwing up myself.

"What happened when you told Yolanda?" I said.

Owen ducked his head. "I left a note on her desk. She hasn't caught up with me yet. But don't you worry about it. I can handle Yo-Yo."

I put my hand over my mouth to hold back a spatter of laughter. He wiggled his eyebrows at me and left.

Thank you for him, God, I thought. *At least he makes me laugh.*

He, in fact, did more than that, I decided as I was fighting my way through the wind out to my car when my shift was over. The way the clouds were scudding across the moon, there was definitely a storm coming up.

It was like Owen was protecting me all the time during work, only I couldn't figure out why. Celeste would have said it was because he had a crush on me, but I doubted that. Owen had mentioned several times that he had a girlfriend—named Genevieve—whom he'd had to promise to capture the moon for this weekend because he'd had to work last weekend. He was acting more like a big brother with me. A big brother with an earring and ever-changing hair.

As I continued speed-walking toward the Volvo, I vaguely wished he and his earring were beside me right that very moment. The empty parking lot was spookier than usual with a storm brewing—like it was stirring up something evil. I had the chilly sensation that there was something waiting in the shadows for me. *Owen's got me all paranoid about Them,* I thought.

I straightened my shoulders with feigned confidence and skittered on.

And then I heard tires squealing. A Jeep came around the corner, and it rocked back and forth, knocking to one side and then the other the head and shoulders of the person who stood up and towered over the roll bar.

Then the head shouted, "Hey baby!" as the Jeep burned its way straight for me.

chaptersix

I couldn't move. It was as if the soles of my shoes were welded to the pavement, and my will to survive right with them. The only sound I could emit was a faint whimper that escaped from somewhere in my nasal cavity—and the only thought I could manage was, I'm going to die! Please—God—don't let me die!

The car was so close by then, I could smell the rubber the driver was leaving behind him. And in spite of my paralyzed state of mind, I could clearly make out the silhouette of a male figure protruding out the top like a gun on an advancing tank.

Yet he couldn't have been real. In my eyes, his square head was larger than a head should be, and his shoulders too, and the ears were waving from the sides of his face like a pair of surreal wings in the wind. It was a monster—how could I save myself from a monster?

There was a sudden pressure on my arm, and for a terror-shocked moment I thought the car had already hit me. Even as I was being yanked from its path and dragged back to the side-walk, I still half-thought I was dead.

Terror struck me. Whoever it was who was holding me—was he part of it? Was he only there to throw me back into the path of the tank—

I started to scream.

"Okay—okay—it's okay," said a deep voice. "I'm not here to hurt you."

I kept my eyes closed as I felt him take his hands away and step back from me. "Do you swear?" I said.

"I promise."

I finally looked up. He was somebody I'd seen before. He was older than I was, though it was hard to tell—as if he didn't really have an age at all. Everything was so unreal.

From a height much taller than me, the young man cocked his head to let the lights behind us shine in my face. It was then I saw the ponytail hanging over his shoulder.

This was Ponytail Boy.

"I just want to see your eyes," he said.

"I think they're seeing things that aren't there," I said.

"Oh, they were definitely there."

"Yeah, but that guy sticking out the top—did he have a head about this big?"

I put my hands out twelve inches from either side of my head. Ponytail Boy's brown eyes smiled.

"He thinks he does." He glanced behind us at a knot of people talking in shrill voices and hurrying stiff-legged toward us from the other end of the parking lot, bent against the wind's gusts, their clothes flapping like flags.

I stiffened against the bricks. "Are they coming back?"

"No, that's your help." Ponytail Boy looked into my face again. "You should never walk out in this parking lot at night by yourself."

"Okay," I said.

The little trio was then upon us. Yolanda was suddenly in my face, Owen was at my elbow, and a security guard was standing in front of me.

They were all talking at once, and I wished Ponytail Boy would just tell them all to go away and leave me alone—that I didn't want to file a police report—that I didn't want to go to the emergency room—that I didn't want to call my parents—that I just wanted to go home and never come back to this heinous place again.

But Ponytail Boy was already gone.

The security guard made me file an incident report, which we did in his car with rain pelting the windshield like thrown gravel. Yolanda darted to her car and then back to ours, soaking-wet cell phone in hand, then tapped on the window to ask yet again if I was all right. The security guard breathed like a locomotive between questions, spewing out the odor of stale cigarettes with every exhalation.

I kept waiting for anxiety to start reappearing, but it didn't.

"Now, you say a fella pulled you out of the path of the vehicle?" Mr. Guard was saying as he consulted his clipboard.

"Yes, sir," I said.

Mr. Guard looked at me, his pen poised above his official-looking form.

"So, what happened to him?" Mr. Guard said.

"I don't know. When all of you got here, he left, I guess."

His prickly brows came together over his nose. "He musta left before that, because I never saw him."

This wasn't the first time something like this had happened. Last fall I'd seen Ponytail Boy for the first time during Trent's fight incident, and later in the semester he'd prompted Joy Beth to come help me when that Shayla girl was getting ready to use me for a punching bag. And the fact that Ponytail Boy was drop-dead stunning, but Celeste didn't know him—that alone was strange enough.

"Do you remember anything else about the males in the vehicle— or the vehicle itself?" Mr. Guard said. "No license plate number?"

I shook my head. I'd already told him that all I knew about the car was that it had been a Jeep with the top off—and all I knew about the boy was that he was big. I had elected not to mention the surrealistic ears and giant head.

By now, my eyelids were pleasantly heavy, and I was wondering vaguely if I were going to be able to drive. Oddly, it wasn't a scary thought. Nothing was scary now. The bad guys were gone, and I just wanted to crawl into bed.

Mr. Guard finally offered me the form, which I signed.

"I'll drive you to your vehicle," he said, "and that young man there in the red Honda is going to follow you home." He was pointing to Owen's car, with Owen in it.

"You be careful in this weather now," Mr. Guard said as he pulled up next to the Volvo. "You've been through enough for this evening."

But as I slid—damply—into my driver's seat, I didn't feel as if I'd been "through" anything at all. I was calm to the very marrow. I waved to Owen and eased the Volvo out onto Route 77.

We got to my house without incident, and Owen's headlights shimmered reassuringly on my wet rear window the whole way. By then the rain was coming down in sheets, and the palm trees in the Cove were bent over like old ladies. I motioned for Owen to go on, but he still waited until I was inside the house before he left. I watched to make sure he and his red Honda didn't float away.

"Who was that?"

I jumped. My dad was sitting at the kitchen table in his pajamas, holding a coffee mug.

"You didn't have to wait up, Dad," I said.

"I think I did. You're about an hour late, and with this storm—"

"I'm okay," I said. "Something happened in the—"

"They're calling for flash floods—winds up to 90 miles an hour. It's not like you're driving an SUV." He got up and dumped the contents of the mug into the sink. "You call if you're going to be late. Your mother worries."

I glanced at the hand that was washing out the cup. Even the coarse dark hairs on his fingers were trembling. And you DON'T worry? I thought. I decided to wait until the next day to tell him about the "incident" in the parking lot—the one that right now I was sleepily wondering if it had really happened.

I kissed my father on the cheek, and stubble prickled at my lips.

"G'night, Baby Girl," Dad said. He couldn't seem to look at me as he let this hand graze my shoulder and went off down the hall.

As soon as I hit my bed, I disappeared into a dreamless sleep that left homework assignments undone and parking lot incidents forgotten.

The crash at two o'clock in the morning was loud enough to wrench me out of that state of oblivion. I lay there for a tangled-up moment until I heard Bonnie scream and Mom stumble down the hall past my door calling out, "What was that? Dear God, what was that?"

That was my question as I struggled out from under the covers and ran for the door. Dad plastered himself in front of it.

"Don't come out here barefoot," he said. "We've got a window broken."

With visions in my head of a Jeep with the top off now parked in our living room amid shards of glass, I jammed my feet into the first shoes I could locate in the bottom of my closet and tore down the hall. Mom was standing at the end of it, holding Bonnie in her arms. Their hair blew straight back, and a mist hit my face as I joined them. We might as well have been standing out in the front yard.

We practically were. Our entire living room window—a large one that took up almost the whole front wall—had been smashed. And the top of a pine tree lay where the sofa had once been. It was now in two chintz pieces, its stuffy insides tearing loose in the wind.

"You girls go in the kitchen," Dad barked at us. "Stay away from this glass."

"What happened, Mommy?" Bonnie was wailing.

Mom didn't answer. I steered her toward the kitchen with Bonnie still demanding answers. When the lights went out and plunged us into darkness, all three of us screamed—and Dad yelled for us to please not become hysterical. We put our arms around each other and stood there in the middle of the kitchen floor, until I started laughing.

"This is not funny, Laura Ann!" Mom said.

"It is when you consider I'm standing here in flannel PJs and black suede pumps," I said.

She sagged against me, squeezing Bonnie between us.

"Ouch!" Bonnie said. "I'm a sandwich! Now tell me what HAPPENED, Mommy?"

We were up for the rest of the night. Our next-door neighbor used the winch on the front of his truck to pull the tree top out of our living room so Dad could board up the window. The quiet that descended once the plywood was finally in place put Bonnie back to sleep with her legs still wrapped around my waist and her drool soaking my chest. I had taken over holding her, while Mom moved furniture away from the windows in all the other rooms and gathered up all her photo albums in case we had to evacuate.

If we do, we're going to need an ark, I thought.

The fallen pine tree had also wreaked some havoc on our roof, and water was pouring into the buckets and dishpans and kitchen pots Mom had scattered all over the living room. I was imagining St. Andrew's Bay, just a few blocks away, smashing against the wall where I often sat with my legs dangling during the quiet times that now seemed so far away. The whipping, raging, furious world I'd experienced tonight made it seem impossible that those times of peace and calm could ever have been.

By dawn the rain had lessened to a solid gray downpour, and the wind gave only the occasional angry gust, as if to remind us that we were still helpless against its unpredictable nature. We didn't have any electricity yet, but Dad resurrected an old transistor radio. The good news was schools were closed for the day; the bad news—several houses out on Bay Pointe had been destroyed by falling trees, slamming waves, and electrical fires.

"That's such a shame," Mom said. "There are some beautiful homes out there."

"They're rich," Dad said. "They can rebuild."

"We can, too, can't we?" I said.

His face was looking lined and strained, and he ran his hand back over the hair that was going in eight different directions.

"We've got insurance, if that's what you mean. But we've got a what—hon?—a $500 deductible?"

Mom nodded soberly.

A stab of guilt came at me from nowhere. If I hadn't messed up my car, they'd still have that $500 in the bank.

Around six a.m., Mom told me to go on to bed. I gratefully crawled beneath the covers, only to be awakened about an hour later by a husky New York accent saying, "Duf-fy…time to wake up."

I pulled my pillow over my head. "What are you doing here?" I moaned. "It's too early for company!"

"I brought your parents coffee. My dad has a generator."

I dug my head deeper under the pillow with my eyes still squeezed shut.

"I brought us hot chocolate," Celeste said. "Unless of course you're too lazy to drag your hind end out of bed—in which case I will be glad to wake up Bonnie and give her your share."

I bolted up. "Wake her up and I'll rip your nose hairs out."

"Real nice, Duffy."

"She was up half the night going, 'What happened, Mommy? What happened, Mommy?'"

"I don't blame her. The front of your house is gone!"

I sat up and made room for both of them on the bed. Joy Beth hoisted herself up.

Celeste produced a thermos and two mugs and started pouring. Heavenly steam rose in the air.

"How's your houses?" I said.

"My dad lost a classic Mustang," Celeste said. "That's all, though."

I had a feeling Mr. Mancini would rather have sacrificed his entire roof than that vintage car.

"I don't know," I said. "Nobody really knows that. Besides—" I took a searing sip out of my cup, "Since a tree fell on my house, does that mean God wanted us to have damage? I don't think it works that way."

"Then how does it work?" she said.

"All I know is that when something bad does happen, God's there to help us through it. And when we get through it, we're stronger and better and wiser and all that because of God. It's like we get power from it."

Besides, a lot of other people got it much worse than we did—"

"You talking about out on Bay Pointe?" Celeste said.

"That's what I heard on the radio. It's really sad."

"It is—but—"

I looked quickly at Celeste. She was studying the foam on her hot chocolate.

"But what?" I said.

"Nothin'. If I say it, I'll sound mean. I hate being mean."

"What's mean is when you start to say something and then leave me hanging—

"Okay—so, like, I know some people who live on Bay Pointe, if you wanna talk about mean. You know some of them, too."

"Like who?" I said.

"Like Virginia Palmer, for openers—that snobby chick that showed up the day you had your car accident."

"You mean Gigi?"

"There's her—and that girl who's playing Patty in your play—I think her name's—"

"Natalie McNair."

"Her father owns a bunch of condos down at the beach. She wears designer underpants for Pete's sake."

"What about Stevie—Stephanie—the other girl they hang out with?" I said.

"She and Natalie are next-door neighbors. I don't know much about her, except personally I think Natalie and Gigi hang out with her because she's a giant guy magnet." It was Celeste's turn to grunt. "Stevie. Her parents must have been big-time Fleetwood Mac fans."

"So I guess Wendy lives out on the Pointe, too," I said.

"Wendy? You mean, Gap Girl Wendy?"

"Yeah. They always come in the store to see her. Last night she pretended she was sick so they could all go hang out together."

"How generous of them to stoop to Wendy's level."

I was a little startled. It was one of the few times I'd ever heard bitterness creep into Celeste's voice.

"Wendy lives around the corner from me, if that tells you anything," Celeste said. "Her father's a welder—but Wendy tries to make like he's some kinda CEO. I hate it when people do that.

What's wrong with just being who you are?"

"Well, I can tell you this much," I said. "Wendy needs God, or she'll never really know who she is."

I felt something warm take shape in me, as if the calm from last night was settling right inside my chest. What I'd just said hadn't come from me. I had a feeling the whisper had skipped my mind altogether and come straight out through my mouth.

Celeste set her cup on my dresser and got into a cross-legged position on the bed. "Okay, so speaking of God, then—you don't think He punishes people sometimes, like, for treating people like they're pond scum?"

"You mean, like tear up their houses with a storm?"

"Yeah—you know—teach them a lesson."

She was genuinely waiting for an answer.

"If they've lost a lot of their stuff, they're going to have to focus on different things. When I had to do that, in a way, that's when I started focusing big-time on God."

"But you don't think God did that to them just so they'd learn that?"

I shook my head hard. "No," I said. "I don't."

Celeste gave a sniff. "But you can't, like, really think girls like Gigi are actually going to turn to God now."

"It's not impossible," I said. "But it probably won't happen—not unless somebody points it out to them."

Celeste narrowed her eyes at me. "Don't try it, Laura. I'm so not kidding you right now. Those girls might be all cute and every-thing, but they can be vicious when they don't get their way. This is no time to play Billy Graham."

"Like I would!"

So am I, like, doomed because I was wishing it was God's punishment when their mansions got washed out into the Bay?"

"No, you're not doomed!"

Celeste flopped onto her back. "That's a relief. Hey—" She sat up again. "Can I go wake up Bonnie now? I want her to have some hot chocolate before it gets cold."

"Do it, and so help me I'll rip your lips off!"

A pillow fight ensued. During it, I watched her out of the corner of my eye, and this time I could practically see her thoughts. They were like dwarves, digging fiercely in the ground. Digging for treasure. Digging for keys.

chapter seven

It was three days before school opened again, and two before I had to go back to the Gap, or, as my father put it, "the salt mines." I'd have preferred the mines, actually, even though I had no idea what they were.

Anyway, I used the time to get as far ahead as I could on homework; I even called my chemistry tutor, Trent Newell, for some over-the-phone tutoring. Too bad the electricity was off because Trent and I actually "talked" more easily via instant messages on the Internet.

I also took the time-off opportunity to practice the chorus songs from *Grease*. Dad rolled the piano into the family room, and every afternoon I sat there singing the opening chorus until I could have done it in my sleep. Bonnie could too, seeing how she sat next to me on the bench and parroted everything I did in her chirpy little voice.

One day Deidre came over and did her alto part with my

soprano, between fits of giggling and conversations that covered everything from the hair that sprouted out of our chemistry teacher's ears to how fabulous it was going to be if we got principal roles in next year's musical.

"It isn't 'if' for you," Deidre said. "It's 'when'."

That felt good.

In fact, a lot of things were feeling good. They felt so good that the day before we went back to school, I actually had a chance for some quiet time OUTSIDE the house. Even as chilly as it was, I wanted to drive out to St. Andrew's State Park, but there were still too many trees and electrical lines down for Dad to let me even take the Volvo out of the driveway. So I stuck my Bible, my journal, and my jacket into my backpack, and wandered on foot the few blocks down to my spot on the Bay.

My stone bench was still there, but there was a five-inch layer of mud on it. The sidewalk was littered with palm fronds, hunks of wood, and debris. There was no place to sit, so I just walked; and the more I walked, the more the calm, warm clarity hardened into a chilled ache in my chest. Most of the mansions along Beach Drive had boards over their previously elegant picture windows. In the marina, sailboats were tumbled on top of each other as if some monstrous child had rifled through his toy box.

It was my first Florida storm, and the devastation of just one night's raging wind and roiling water stunned me to the core.

Things that had seemed so solid were in pieces around me. What if surrendering without the next key left things broken and scattered?

The backpack was suddenly heavy on my shoulders. Was the FIRST key even helping? I was surrendering my head off, but it wasn't changing anything, not the way it used to. Sure, the storm had given me a chance to get caught up, but there was still all this stuff I either couldn't get out of or didn't want to get out of—

My job. Worrying about the car. Trying to keep my grades up with all the other stuff I had to do.

Helping Joy Beth. Figuring out how I was going to get out of work for the nighttime tech rehearsals What about the next key?

Unexpected tears suddenly blurred my vision, and I had to stop and lean against the railing. I HAD to know, I had to find it—and it wasn't just for me. It was for my friends, too.

I need Mrs. Isaacsen, I thought.

Her card was still in the zipper pocket of my backpack. So much had happened since Monday, I hadn't even opened it. I was openly grinning-with-hope as I pulled out the card. With it came another envelope—the parchment one.

I tucked Mrs. I.'s envelope in my armpit and opened the Secret Admirer's note to read it again:

> *Fill this with priceless treasures.*
> *I know you can.*

Although I'd moved the treasure chest in my locker about a half dozen times since it had appeared, this was the first time I'd really thought much about it since then.

Before, several months ago, when the Secret Admirer had left a grapevine that somehow grew on the outside of my locker, it turned out to symbolize something—something I couldn't exactly describe—that had enriched me, put me at peace. But this time, giving me a chest I couldn't open and telling me to fill it with priceless treasures when I didn't have two dimes to rub together seemed almost cruel.

"I don't know who you are," I whispered. "But you sure don't know what's going on in *my* life. If I *had* any treasures, I'd sell them and pay back my father!"

I was annoyed all of a sudden. Why did this person have to be so cryptic? If he liked me, why didn't he just ask me out like any sane person would do? And if he just wanted to be friends, he could come to our lunch table and mooch off my chocolate chip cookies or something normal, instead of playing these head games.

I stuffed the note away and retrieved Mrs. Isaacsen's. The second it was out of the envelope, I was grinning again. It was one of those cards for little kids where inanimate objects do human stuff and five year olds think it's hilarious. This one showed a heart with arms, legs, and a face, standing on a stage and singing with her mouth open so wide I could see pink tonsils. On the inside it said: *You make my heart sing.*

I let out a large guffaw, but my laughter died when I read what Mrs. Isaacsen had written:

Laura,

My heart does sing when I watch you turn your attention to the true treasures of your world. Thank you for sometimes letting me help you dig for them.

Mrs. I.

I went cold.

I'd thought once before that Mrs. Isaacsen was my Secret

Admirer. Everything had pointed to her at that time, but she'd convinced me that she wasn't and I'd believed her. She wouldn't lie to me.

I thrust her card into the backpack with the other one. *But she knows who it is,* I told myself. *They're coordinating their messages, for Pete's sake! How else could this happen—again?*

I slung my pack over one shoulder and marched toward home.

* * * * * *

Dad insisted on taking me to work that night and said for me to call him when I was ready to come home.

When I got to the break room to clock in, Wendy's face was raw-looking and puffed up, and her eye make-up had disappeared. She must REALLY be upset to let that happen.

Owen came in behind me and checked her out even as he was pulling out his cards.

"What's up with you?" he said. "You look terrible."

She went for her purse and pulled out a compact.

"You okay?" I said.

"No," she said. "I just found out one of my best friends is moving away."

"Oh," I said. I sank into the chair across the table from her. "I'm sorry. I hate that."

Wendy gazed into the mirror. I could feel Owen standing behind me, and I could imagine him rolling his eyes.

"I look terrible," Wendy said. "I shouldn't even be here."

"You could always go make yourself puke so you could go home," Owen said cheerfully.

"Shut up." Her eyes shifted to me. "You did tell Yolanda I was sick the other night, didn't you?"

"No, I did," Owen said. "And can I just say that was pretty low—getting Laura to do it when you knew she'd get in trouble?"

"You can say it, but nobody's listening." Wendy scraped back her chair. "I'm stocking shelves tonight. I don't feel like dealing with customers."

"Lucky for the customers," Owen said when the door had closed behind her. He turned to me. "I'm surprised to even see you here. I thought maybe your parents wouldn't let you come back to work after what happened the other night."

"I didn't tell them."

"Ya'll are close, then."

"No! I mean, yes, we are pretty close. But we had some damage— " Two minutes later I was still talking. And Owen was still sitting there, watching me and nodding.

"Y'know, you can just tell me to shut up anytime," I said. "Have you ever thought about being a counselor? You're a really good listener."

"As if I could counsel anybody—screwed up as I am," he said. "I do want to ask you something about that thing in the parking lot though."

"I don't remember that much. It happened so fast."

"You sure you don't remember, like, what the guy in the Jeep looked like?"

I pulled my eyes away.

"So you do remember. Look, if you're trying to protect some-body…"

"It's not that! It's just that what I remember is so weird—you'll think I'm a psycho."

"I'm not gonna think you're a psycho. Tell me." He sat back.

I lowered my voice and told him about the head like a big square box and elephant ears flapping like they were under water.

He was staring at me. "You're right," he said. "I think you're a psycho."

"I told you!"

"I'm kidding!."

He leaned back in the chair again, hands behind his head. I noticed that his hair was now raven-black. Forget working to put himself through college; he was obviously spending all of his paychecks on hair dye.

"I do know a little psychology," he said. "My mom used to be a psychiatric aide."

"See!"

"She's told me stories about some weird stuff. Like when people get freaked out, sometimes they see things distorted, except there's a grain of truth to them."

"I don't get it."

Owen dug into his other pocket and pulled out a small pad of paper. A pencil came out from behind his ear.

"Let's say the guy did have a square head, only it wasn't 800 cubic inches or whatever. It was more like this—"

Owen deftly drew a male head, square but without features. I was the one staring now.

"You're an artist," I said.

"Yeah, well, whatever—and let's say our boy has bigger than average ears, but not like Dumbo. Say they're this size, coming out from his head some—"

I watched in amazement as protruding ears came into view.

"Maybe they looked big because his hair was cut short." He grinned at me. "You didn't see a big bloody mane streaming out or anything, did you?"

"No. I didn't see hair at all."

"If he'd had hair it would have been doing something in that wind."

"Yeah," I said. "You'd think so."

"So let's give Bad Boy a buzz cut. Now, you don't recall anything about His Badness's mouth?"

"It was open. It was square, too. I don't know, like hard."

"Uh-huh." The picture grew beneath his pencil lead. "Eyes?"

"No. I couldn't see his eyes."

"Well, I bet they weren't the picture of compassion." He continued to shade as I watched.

"*Voilà!*" he said. Owen turned the drawing around so I could stare it full in the face. I felt my eyes popping.

"You know him," Owen said.

I forced a smile against an unwelcome thought that was taking shape in my head. "Every boy at 'Nama looks like that."

"Do they?" I felt Owen's fingers under my chin, lifting it up. "You know who this is."

"I know who it *could* be," I said slowly. "But that isn't enough to tell the cops or something! What if it isn't him? That would be SO bad."

"I'm not saying tell the police. I'm saying protect yourself."

"I am! The guy who saved me that night told me not to go in the parking lot by myself, and I won't. And you know what else? I'm not sure he even 'saved' me. Those guys were just out messing around, probably drunk. It wasn't like they were really going to run me over. Maybe they were just trying to freak me out—and not me personally, but just me-because-I-happened-to-be-there."

Owen had taken the drawing back and was shading intaut tendons in the cheekbones.

"Just think about it. If you do suspect for a second that Mr. Bad here has it in for you for some reason, just watch your back."

I put my hands over my mouth as he slid the drawing back to me. Owen had to know him, too, or he couldn't have drawn the spitting image of Vance Woodruff. The only thing missing from the picture was the black Silverado.

chapter eight

F or the rest of my shift, I concentrated on denying the possibility that Vance Woodruff and his band of rich buddies would actually come after me for damaging Vance's precious vehicle. It was already paid for—so why would he still be mad?

I bet I PUT that monster face on Bad Boy in my imagination because I still feel guilty about messing up Vance's truck, I told myself at about four a.m. And now I'm going to forget about him and his friends and the Gap Girls and concentrate on something that matters.

Of course, the next day at school, there was nothing BUT talk about the storm damage. It became the topic of conversation in our group.

"I heard that a couple of kids lost, like, everything," Celeste said.

"Gigi Palmer's house caught on fire because of some electrical thing," K.J. said matter-of-factly, "Her family's got practically nothing now. And Natalie McNair's? A tree fell right in the middle of their house."

"Was anybody hurt?" I said.

"No, but they're out of here." She jerked a thumb in a northerly direction. "They're moving up to Nashville."

Mrs. Isaacsen was looking at K.J. with her eyebrows pulled in toward the bridge of her nose. "How on earth do you get your information, child? I didn't know half of that, and we had a briefing at the staff meeting this morning."

"I have ways," K.J. said.

"That's just sad," Celeste said. "I mean, think about losing everything you have."

I found myself staring at Celeste. This was a different tune than she'd been singing in my room the day after the storm. Maybe she HAD listened to me.

"They'll live," somebody else said.

We all turned to look at Michelle, who was sitting all the way back in her chair, fiddling with a hoop earring Her face was almost expressionless.

"Let's see where this takes us," Mrs. Isaacsen said. "Do you want to elaborate on that, Michelle?"

"No. I just think it's obvious: they lost THINGS. They have money. They'll get their THINGS back."

By now she was pulling so hard on the earring, I was afraid she would rip out the pierce-hole.

"So, THINGS don't mean that much to you?" Mrs. Isaacsen said.

"They mean nothing to me."

"Get outa town!" Celeste said. "I mean, really—you don't own, like, anything that would make you flip out if you lost it?"

"I don't 'flip out'," Michelle said.

"So—Celeste—what about you?" Mrs. Isaacsen said. "How much do material things mean to you?"

Celeste looked down at the plaid kilt she was wearing with knee socks and a jean jacket. "I like to collect weird stuff—but I can always go back to Good Will and find more." Her face eased into a smile, as if she were making a discovery. "I guess I'm not as tied up in 'stuff' as I thought I was. I'm really about my friends, you know? What would flip me out would be if something happened to Laura or Joy Beth."

She turned her eyes to me, and I could feel her love flowing straight into me, pressing against my guilt. I still hadn't told her about the parking lot incident. And now I knew I wasn't going to. She would want to go hunt down Bad Boy and probably get us both mowed down—or worse, if it really HAD been Vance...

"Let's regroup." Mrs. Isaacsen said.. "The way we view material things says a lot about what's truly important to us. What you treasure is where your heart is."

There it is again, I thought. *That treasure thing*. I squirmed.

"I'd like for ya'll to examine that a little further for next time," Mrs. I. said.

As we all got up to leave, she whispered to me, "You want to come see me after rehearsal? I'll still be here."

I nodded. Maybe the way to get back the warmth and the calm was to find out what she and my Secret Admirer were really trying to tell me.

Right after music theory class that afternoon, Mr. Howitch said he wanted to talk to me before rehearsal. I did my usual paranoid what-am-I-in-trouble-for mental debate all last period, but I couldn't come up with anything.

The only thing that interrupted those thoughts was my quick trip to my locker. I opened the door, and something flew out into my face. I squealed, attracting Mr. Real World's attention from above.

"What?" he said.

"Nothing," I said. It was just a moth. What it was doing in my locker, I had no idea, but I swatted at air and stuck my head in again. I had to move the treasure chest to dig out my copy of *Gatsby*, and when I did, something came off on my hand, something gritty.

How's it getting dirty? I thought. *It's been in here the whole time.*

I knew I should probably get the chest out of there, but I wasn't sure what to do with it. I was about to just wipe my hand on the front of my jacket when I saw that whatever it was had a red tinge to it.

"What the—?" I said.

"Dude, you got something rustin' down there," Real World said. "Get some Rustoleum."

"Thanks," I muttered.

Terrific. Now my locker was rusting out. But I didn't have time to worry about it now. I needed to get to Mr. Howitch before the suspense drove me nuts.

By the time I arrived at his office adjacent to the choir room, I was having heart palpitations. I felt like a schizophrenic, lurching from annoyance to guilt to calm and then to near panic, like I had about seven different personalities.

There were several people in the choir room, huddled in a group that I only saw out of the corner of my eye as I honed in on Mr. Howitch, bent over his desk on the other side of the window that separated his office from the room. Still, their presence introduced a whole new set of possibilities.

Maybe he has to cut down the show because we missed so much rehearsal time. Maybe these are all the people he's taking out. Maybe that's why it feels so tense in here.

I started to tap on the door, just as I thought, *Maybe I'm one of them.*

I looked behind me at the huddle. "Are you guys waiting to see him? Do I need to take a number or something?"

A now-familiar face turned to me, startling me with its presence in a room where it didn't belong. There was a chill in Gigi's eyes.

"No," she said icily.

Then she turned back to her group and exchanged contemptuous glances with Wendy.

Wendy?

What the heck are THEY doing in here? I thought. *They're not even IN the music program.*

Good grief—until about two weeks ago I hadn't even known their names. Now I was falling over Them every time I turned around. Who else was over there hiding behind them—

"Laura!" said a voice behind me. I gave a startled jolt as Mr. Howitch, now standing behind me with the door open, touched my elbow and motioned me inside.

I felt my heart trying to dislodge itself as I followed him into the office.

He moved a stack of sheet music off a chair. "Thanks for coming in, Laura." he perched on the very edge of his desk in front of me.

"Would you be willing to help me out with something?" he said.

"Yes, sir," I said. Just don't ask me to drop out of the show. *PLEASE— I'll do ANYTHING else. I'll swing from the fly rail—*

He got up and twisted the plastic rod on the window blinds so we were slowly cut off from the view of the Gap Group in the chorus room.

THAT can't be good, I thought. Now I wished he'd just drop the axe across my neck and get it over with.

"The way the rumor mill churns around here," Mr. Howitch said when he was re-perched, "I'm sure you've already heard that Natalie McNair is moving out of the area."

"I did hear that." Something stirred in my mind—something I would have realized earlier if I hadn't been so wrapped up in my ever-changing emotions.

"That leaves us without a Patty," Mr. Howitch said. "My first choice for someone to replace her is you. How would you feel about taking that on?"

All I could do was gape at him as if I'd lost all muscle tone in my face. If the role of Patty had called for a mute, I'd have been his ONLY choice.

"Um—yeah—" I said finally, and eloquently. "I'd love to do it!"

Mr. Howitch smiled, "Now, before you commit, I want you to know that it's going to take extra practice time in addition to our regular rehearsals to bring you up to speed. How are your activity periods?"

"They're free! I mean, they CAN be. Mrs. Isaacsen has a group that meets Tuesdays and Thursdays, and—"

"It would only be temporary. I know you're a quick study—you'll BE Rizzo by tomorrow afternoon most likely. You check it out with Mrs. Isaacsen. Do I need to put in a good word—?"

"No," I said quickly. "I'll take care of it."

I was sure Mrs. Isaacsen was going to turn cartwheels for me.

"Here's a script with all the blocking written in the margins," Mr. Howitch said.

"I'll have my lines learned by tomorrow," I said.

"A week from today is fine. But the sooner you can fit into the scenes we've already rehearsed, the better."

"I'm going to work really hard," I said. "I can come in before school if you want—and I can stay a little while after rehearsal, especially on Tuesdays and Thursdays because I don't work those nights—"

"You work, too?" he said.

"Only three nights a week," I said. "And one weekend day." I shrugged my shoulders right up to my ear lobes. "It's not that big a deal, really."

"What about tech rehearsal week?" His eyes were beady, as if he'd found some weakness in an alibi.

"I'm going to get those nights off," I said—a decision I made on the spot. "The show comes first, Mr. Howitch, whether I'm Rizzo or still a member of the chorus. This is the most important thing in my life right now—"

Is it? Are you sure?

I turned to the whisper—and then I glanced quickly back at Mr. Howitch. For a frozen second I thought he'd heard it, too.

"It's who I AM!" I said to both voices. "I just focus on this—

and, you know, my grades—"

The twinkle was back in his eyes. "Just as long as you have your priorities straight. But re-think whether you really need to work next year because I plan to keep you busy around here."

He could have told me I was destined for Broadway and I would-n't have felt a bigger thrill.

I stayed thrilled throughout rehearsal, especially with everybody coming up and whispering congratulations to me during breaks. I stayed after to run some lines with The Pink Ladies—my onstage gang—and belted out every song in the whole show all the way home.

I couldn't wait to tell Mom and Bonnie my news, and after that, while I was taking a shower, they still managed to put together a "Way to Go, Laura!" banner and decorate a big star-shaped cookie. Mom kept dough in the freezer for just such occasions, though since we'd moved to Florida, most of them had been for Bonnie. This was my first really big accomplishment in our new life, and as I drove to work, munching away on my stardom, I had to admit it felt good to be basking in parental admiration again.

I was disappointed that Owen wasn't working that night, but I didn't have to close. I couldn't wait to meet Celeste and Joy Beth and Trent at Books-A-Million after my shift and telling them the news. It was enough to get me through a woman returning a pair of low-rise jeans she said we should never have "let" her four-teen-year-old daughter buy in the first place AND Yolanda putting me on dressing room duty for the first time and teaching me how to police for shoplifters. Nothing could shake me, now that I was being allowed to prove myself to Mr. Howitch and the entire musical world. My circuits were definitely still loaded.

Until somebody pulled the plug—and everything went cold.

chapter nine

It was all I could do to force myself to go back to the Gap after my break that night, but I did want to talk to Yolanda so I could get the dates of my time-off-for-tech-week on her calendar. She was busy with a customer when I got back, though, and since Owen wasn't there to force me to take my entire break, I returned to the dressing room duty early.

It was quiet in the area. In fact, even Wendy wasn't back there, and I assumed she was returning stuff to the racks—although from the looks of the Reject Rack behind me, nobody had done it all evening. I glanced nervously out into the store for Yolanda. We were getting toward the end of our shift. It should have been done by now, and Wendy had assured me she would take care of it.

I took another anxious glance, this time down the aisle between the two rows of dressing rooms. There were no numbers hanging on doors, which meant nobody was even trying on—so why wasn't Wendy restocking?

And why did I hear hissing voices coming from the far end, like there was more than one person in a dressing room? That was a mortal sin in Gap Land. One of the employees had to have put the customers in there, since the doors were kept locked otherwise— unless the customers had doubled up when Wendy wasn't looking. But somebody was always supposed to be looking.

Glancing warily in all directions this time, I crept quietly down the aisle toward the whispers. Yolanda's instructions were ticking off in my head.

Count the customer's items and put the corresponding number tag on the outside of the dressing room door.

No more than four items at a time.

No more than one teenager in a dressing room.

Okay, this has got to be some kind of test, I thought—as I began to dehydrate. Nobody would be this obvious. It's like Yolanda wants to see if I'll catch them and turn them in.

But did Yolanda do stuff like that? Owen had never mentioned it. Where was he when I needed him, anyway?

I stopped two booths away from the voices.

"This doesn't make me look fat?" Voice Number One whispered.

"Are you serious? You're a stick," said Voice Number Two.

"It pulls right here." "Well, that's because you have humungous boobs."

There was a giggle, which was immediately hushed by a "SHHH!"

Once again you have been taken hostage by your imagination, Duffy, I told myself. *Just go get Wendy and find out why there's no hanger on the door—*

And then it came. A third whisper-voice from the dressing room.

"So hurry up," said Voice Number Three. "Which one do you want? She's gonna be back, like, any minute."

"I want them both," hissed Voice Number One.

"You can't. It'll be too obvious," Three whispered.

"But this is my last chance. It's not like you can do this for me when I move three hundred and fifty miles away."

"I just don't think I can get away with two of them."

"So make Yolanda think that new girl did it." That came from Voice Number Two, a chilly voice I couldn't have mistaken if it had been distorted by helium. It was Gigi.

"Like she'd believe it," Voice Three whispered. "Yolanda thinks she's an angel."

"Who doesn't? Howitch is like in love with her." Voice Two had ceased even trying to be quiet, but it wouldn't have mattered.

The bitterness alone told me it was Natalie. So Voice Number Three had to be Wendy.

"Just pick ONE—okay? Please?" it said. "Maybe I can do more before you move—"

"Fine. This one."

"Give me the rejects."

The rattle of hangers broke me out of my paralysis long enough to get me back to my work station. A woman in her twenties was there, holding a pair of white Capri pants and glancing at her watch.

"I'm sorry!" I said in a voice loud enough to be heard at the Tallahassee store. "You shouldn't have had to wait! How many items do you have, ma'am?"

The woman looked immediately amused. "Just one. You know, it's nice to see somebody who actually LIKES her job."

"Love it!" I sang out.

I felt like an idiot, but at least I'd produced the desired result. As I led Ms. Capris to a dressing room, Wendy slipped out and hurried past me with at least ten pastel tops in tow.

"No luck, huh?" I said.

"What?" she said. She didn't stop or look over her shoulder as I followed her to the dressing area counting desk.

"They sent a lot of stuff back out." I tried to do a quick count of the tops with my eyes, even as Wendy grabbed several items off the rack and loaded them on top of her already high pile, so that I could barely see her chin. "I thought we were only supposed to let them go in with four items."

Wendy seemed to go pale as she finally stopped moving. "You're still in training," she said. "They haven't made you dressing-room monitor yet."

"Sorry," I said. "I was just making sure—"

She lowered her voice to her previous clandestine whisper. "When it's somebody you can trust, you can bend the rules.".

"Oh," I said. "So, you don't have to put an item count on their door either?"

She went even paler, and I knew now that it wasn't a figment I'd conjured. "I guess you're supposed to," Wendy said. "I didn't even think about it. You don't have to report this to Yolanda, though."

She delivered that suggestion like it was written in the employees' manual, and it seethed under my skin.

You really think I'm clueless, don't you? I wanted to say to her.

Do you think just because I'm not one of You, I don't have a brain in my head?

It must have shown on my face, because for a second Wendy looked surprised, just before she rolled her eyes and turned to march off with the armload of merchandise. She plowed straight into Yolanda.

"Hello!" Yolanda said. "Careful there!"

I didn't have to glance behind me to know that Capri Woman had come out of the dressing room and was witnessing the scene. Otherwise, Yolanda would have let Wendy have it. As it was, she took some of the stuff off of Wendy's hands and walked with her out onto the floor, and I could see her spitting under-her-breath phrases into Wendy's left ear.

"I'm going to take these," Capri Woman said.

"Great!" I said. "Can we help you find some tops to go with them?"

She put a tanned hand on my arm. "Honey, if I needed tops, you'd be the first person I'd come to. Thanks for making my day."

When she'd gone off toward the checkout counter, a well-chilled voice said beside me, "Well, aren't you just the little Sales Girl of the Month?"

I looked quickly at Gigi, but there was no sarcasm in her eyes. There was only the calm, assured look of someone who has it all and knows she can get more. There was no need to waste energy on me.

But then she did.

"Listen," she said. "Can we talk later? Will you be working this weekend?"

"Sunday," I said woodenly. I might not have answered her at all if I hadn't been caught completely off guard.

Natalie emerged then, and wthout a word, she walked past. But the look she delivered could have sliced a ham. They both , exited into the mall. Neither of them so much as looked for Wendy.

Shoplifting had taken place, I was sure of that—even though I couldn't prove it. Gigi and Natalie had both been carrying shoulder bags that were barely big enough to hold their daddies' Gold Cards, but that didn't mean Natalie hadn't absconded with at least one top.

They'll try to get out with new merchandise under their clothes, Yolanda had told me. Which was why they put those big plastic alarms on everything but the sale stuff.

And everything Wendy had carried out of the dressing room

had come from the sale table.

One thing was for sure: the minute my shift was over, I got out of there, leaving Wendy to close with Yolanda and a couple of other people. Wendy even reminded me that I didn't have to stay, and I knew it was because she didn't want me to be alone with Yolanda. Even though I did need to talk to her about time off for tech week, I decided my next shift would be soon enough. I needed to get to my friends before I went nuts.

That night at Books-A-Million could have been Kids-A-Million. The it's-too-early-for-the-parties crowd was staking their claim in the coffee shop with five small tables pushed together around two stuffed chairs sitting near the window to accommodate them all.

The wonderful combination smell of new books and freshly brewed coffee had a sophistication I loved. Celeste waved to me from a tiny table she'd rescued, and when I got there, she and Joy Beth already had a café mocha waiting for me—and a gift bag spewing pink tissue paper.

"What's this?" I said.

"For you," Celeste said. "Pink like a poodle skirt."

"You know already?" I said. "Who told you?"

"Who didn't?"

Joy Beth grunted and pushed the gift bag toward me. "Congratulations present," she said.

I tore out the poodle-skirt-pink paper and pulled a slim volume from the bag. It was a journal, its cover a mass of stars.

"It's so you can chronicle this whole experience," Celeste said.

"You guys!" I said.

"Break a leg," Joy Beth said.

"Drink up, and then we'll order another round," Celeste said as she tapped her cup against mine. "We are SO celebrating tonight."

"Where's Trent?" I said.

Joy Beth stopped craning her neck toward the door and said, "Late."

I brought my cup to my lips, but across from me, Celeste's eyes flickered above my head and hardened there.

"Can we help you?" she said.

I turned around. Gigi was standing over me.

"I thought you'd want to know that Natalie is right over there," she said.

I glanced toward the mass of people by the window. I couldn't see Natalie, but I could now hear what I thought was probably her, sobbing from the midst of them.

Gigi leveled her ice-blue eyes at me. "I didn't think you were the type to be insensitive."

"We wouldn't have picked this place if we'd known she was going to be here," said Celeste.

"We're here every Friday night around ten," Gigi said, as if that were information we'd want for future reference.

Only so I'll remember NOT to be here, I thought. Was there no way to get away from these people?

"So could I talk to you alone for a minute?" Gigi said to me.

"Whatever you've got to say to her we can hear," Celeste said.

Joy Beth was nodding.

I stood up. "It's okay, you guys. I'll just be a minute."

"We'll be right here if you need us," Celeste said. She looked as if she'd rather be releasing me to a school of sharks.

I'll be fine, I said to her with my eyes. I knew this had to be about the shoplifting thing, and since Gigi was so bent on talking to me, I was bent on getting to the truth.

That didn't mean I wasn't breathing like that coffee bean grinder whining and rattling behind the counter. I followed Gigi to a bench between two shelves of books. She straddled the bench to face me.

"I know Mr. Harowitz didn't tell you this—" Gigi said.

"Who?" I said.

"The chorus guy."

"Howitch," I said.

"Whatever. I know he didn't tell you this, but if you had turned down the part, he was going to let Natalie come back and do it for the performances. Her parents would have flown her down here and everything."

That part I didn't doubt. The rest of it, though—no stinkin' way.

"Why didn't he just let her, then?" I said. "Why did he even ask me?"

"Well because—Natalie told him to do whatever was best for the whole show because that's what's most important."

That would be the first time she ever said anything like that, I thought.

I quickly recalled memories of Natalie still doing act one with a script in her hand the day we were supposed to be "off book" and have all our lines memorized, and Natalie coming in late to rehearsals as if we were all biting our nails in anticipation of her arrival. And what about the time Natalie was loudly complaining about how Sandy was upstaging her, even though Sandy WAS the focus of the scene. I could have remembered vignettes like that all night, but I blinked at Gigi and said, "So he decided that wasn't best for the show."

"Yes and no." She leaned in closer yet. "He said the best thing for the show was for her to stay here, that nobody else could play the role like she's doing it. I mean, come on, she has this Celine Dion voice." I raised my eyebrows. "Anyway," she hurried on, "he said he would have to try to find somebody else who could maybe do half as good a job as Natalie, and if he couldn't—he would let her fly in just for the show."

"It doesn't sound to me like if I said no it was all set for her to do that," I said. "There are other people who could do the role, too."

"All the good people already have roles, Laura," she said.

The sound of my name coming out of her mouth made me shiver inwardly.

"So if you would step down, Natalie could have her part back."

"Why would Natalie want me to do that if she doesn't think it's the best thing for the show?"

"She's just being modest, which is why I'm the one talking to you and not her. Besides, you heard how upset she is."

"Yeah," I said. "I was like that when I had to move, too, so I know what it's like, but—"

"See, I don't really know you," Gigi said, "but other people have told me how decent you are. That's why I knew I could talk to you about this. I know it's a hard decision. I'd have a hard time walking away from something like this, too, if it were me, but I don't think it's going to be that hard for you, once you think about it." She patted my shoulder lightly. "Take until Monday if you have to. Natalie isn't leaving until Wednesday."

Then she got up and returned to her kingdom, while I stopped clenching my hands and started yanking my jacket zipper up and down. Celeste found me sitting there.

"Joy Beth's out there with Trent," she said. "We're moving the celebration someplace else." She squatted down in front of me. "You look like you want to smack somebody. What did she say to you?"

I kept my voice low and tight as I told her. I was afraid if I let go at all, I would bring down both shelves of books. When I was done, Celeste rocked back on her heels, her eyes in slits.

"Well, first of all, Goddess Gigi," she said, "thank you for coming down from On High to deliver your commandments." Celeste's entire upper lip curled. "Who died and left her in charge—'You can have until Monday'—gimme a break!"

"I know I'm not supposed to hate people, but—"

"But she's not a person, Duffy. She's an ice sculpture with an ego problem, okay? You don't believe ANY of that load of garbage, do you?"

I shook my head. "If she knew Mr. Howitch—which she doesn't because she can't even pronounce his name—she wouldn't try to pull that on me."

"You know what it is?" Celeste said. "Natalie can't get her own way and she's throwing a tantrum. None of them can stand not being in total control over everything, so they start trying to move everybody else around like we're all checkers on their checker-board

"They're like McDonald's," I said. "Everywhere I turn, there's another one."

Celeste stood up. I got my first real look at her get-up for the evening.

"Celeste?" I said. "Is that an ascot you're wearing?"

"Yes!" she said. "I wanted to look like a theatre person tonight. Now let's go celebrate." She linked her black-clad arm through mine and led me back toward the coffee shop. "McDonald's doesn't sound like a bad idea—I could so go for some of their fries. And you know what, Duffy, if you had been at the big audition last fall, Mr. Howitch would have cast you as Rizzo in the first place."

She jabbered on and I felt better. At least for a little while.

chapter ten

From the minute I woke up Saturday morning, the shoplifting incident never left my head. And by the time I got to work Sunday afternoon, I had considered and rejected every possible option for dealing with it:

> 1. Go to Yolanda, tell her what I'd heard, and let her take it from there.

> 2. Tell Wendy what I knew and warn her that if the merchandise didn't come back, I was telling Yolanda.

> 3. Quit so I didn't have to deal with it at all.

I prayed, I wrote in my journal, I took a brisk walk by the Bay to clear my head—anything I could think of that might help me make the right decision. I even woke up four or five times during the night and imagined myself holding forth in Yolanda's office or pinning Wendy up against the wall in the break room.

But none of the three scenarios had much going for it. The first one would put me in even deeper with *Them*, and that brought on images of Vance Woodruff running me down with a large tractor-trailer rig. The second option would probably bring the same result. And number three was completely unrealistic. No matter how you looked at it, I still had to pay back my father and he wasn't getting any richer. The insurance company had notified my parents that it wasn't going to give them enough money to restore our living room to its former state, and Dad was talking about getting a second job to make up the difference. Early Sunday morning I'd overheard a tearful conversation between him and Mom. She volunteered to get a job again and Dad growled that he could take care of his family. That emotional scene chased option number three off the list immediately.

When I got to the break room that afternoon, Owen greeted me with a half grin. "Steer clear of Yolanda today. Wendy called in sick and Yo-Yo is *not* happy."

"Thank you, God," I whispered. It gave me an excuse to put off telling Yolanda about Wendy.

Owen frowned at me . "You're not letting this place get to you, are you?"

"I don't have to 'let' it. It's getting to me all on its own."

He patted the chair next to him. "The doctor is in, and he's got a special on today: Five minutes—free."

I opened the floodgates and everything spilled out—from the shoplifting to my "chat" with Gigi at Books-A-Million.

"You could use what you overheard in the dressing room to take down all of Them!" Owen blurted. "They'd do it to you in a second."

"But it would totally be my word against theirs."

"Yolanda would believe you in a second." Owen absently began to sketch in his notepad. "That's what I've learned about you, girl-friend. Anybody else would use their favor with the queen to get Wendy and Their Ladyships strung up by their little waxed eyebrows. But not you. You stay up nights worrying about whether it's the truth or not." Owen looked up from his drawing.

"I'm not some saint, if that's what you're thinking."

He went back to sketching. "Ah. Do I detect a little fear in there?"

"Fear?"

"Look, I wouldn't blame you. One of Their Lords tried to run you down. Face it, they're bullies. Everybody's afraid of them."

My heart stopped, and I stared at the side of his face until my eyes pulled so hard they hurt.

"I knew who I was drawing the other day," he said, pencil scratching across the pad. "I've seen Lord Bad Boy hanging around the store."

"I don't know if it was him," I said. "But I do know that whoever it was that night wasn't waiting for me in particular."

"And you know this how? Listen, people like the ones who run with that crowd are not above doing whatever they have to do to make people cow-tow, you know what I'm saying? When they want something, they get it; and if you are in the way, they get you. Looks to me like you're in their way on a number of levels." Owen glanced up at the clock and slowly unfolded himself to stand up. "If it's fear that's keeping you from telling Yolanda about this, I understand that better than I understand you wanting to be sure you're telling the truth. The truth isn't going to protect you from Them." He handed his drawing to me. The faces of Gigi, Natalie, Wendy, Stevie, and Vance—even Ethan—looked up at me from beneath comical jester hats. Their eyes, however, were not laughing.

The layer of confusion Owen had just added to my decision about what to do about Wendy and her crew weighed me down until I was emotionally bent in half. As I followed him out into the store, it annoyed me in a major way and didn't let go. In fact, it ate away all my warm calm—just chewed it up and spit it right out. I was a basket case again.

* * * * * *

Why am I not allowed to just enjoy the fact that I'm finally getting to do something I really want to do in this school? I thought as I trudged to my locker Monday morning. *Why does it have to get so complicated? It's the stupid job that's messed everything up—*

I gave the combination lock an angry twist and yanked open the door. An off-white envelope tumbled out.

Wonderful, I thought as I snatched it up. *Why don't you just add MORE stuff to my load? Like I really need that from somebody who supposedly admires me—*

But even as I was ranting to myself, I slit the envelope open with my thumb and unfolded the usual parchment note. Its energy forced my fingers, just like it always did.

Beware of thieves who will break in and steal, The Secret Admirer had written this time. *Protect your true treasures.*

Before the words could even settle in, I looked inside my locker for the treasure chest.

But it was gone.

I went cold and looked frantically behind me. All I saw was a field of knees and calves heading to classes. None were darting away as if they'd just stolen something from my locker.

I stared back at the note. Beware of thieves who will break in and steal. It looked like they already had.

I shivered. It was bad enough that my Secret Admirer had access to my locker, but to think somebody else—

Or could it be the same person? Was he driving his message home by taking away the treasure chest he had given to me?

I never even opened it! It was locked! I wanted to scream at him. I don't have time to store up treasures! I can hardly take care of the ones I have!

"What's up, Duff? You look like you're about to hurl."

"No, I'm fine," I said to Celeste."

"NO, you are NOT. Can we talk about this at lunch?"

"I can't—I have to run lines, and after school I've got rehearsall, of course, and I've gotta work tonight..."

Celeste sagged.

"I'll call you the minute I get home from work," I said. "I promise—this is the most important thing—"

"Is it?" she said. I saw desperation in her eyes. "I wanna believe that, Duffy."

It was a good thing we had silent reading in English because all I did was cry behind the covers of *The Great Gatsby*. Ms. Wren came by with a wad of Kleenex and whispered, "It is rather sad, isn't it?" and patted my shoulder.

By the time I got to second period history, I had wiped off all my mascara and blown my nose so many times, I was sure it looked like a cherry tomato.

When the bell rang, and I felt a touch on my shoulder, I jerked up so Mr. Beecher wouldn't think I was napping. My entire face came unhinged when I saw Stevie looking into it.

The mane of highlighted hair fell forward until it almost touched me.

"You okay?" she said.

My surprise turned to suspicion. *You care?* I wanted to say to her. Instead I just nodded.

"Good thing we have a sub today," she said. I noticed that her eyes nearly crinkled closed when she smiled.

Give it up, chick, I thought. *You can try all the tactics you want, but I am NOT giving up my role to Natalie—*

As she continued on to her desk, I felt something surge through me. I hadn't felt this way for months. I watched my fists tighten and felt my teeth clench—and I knew any minute I was likely to hurl my history binder at the substitute.

The only sane thought in my head was: *I've gotta make an appointment to see Mrs. Isaacsen.*

The sub seemed more than happy to write me a pass, as she was sending people to the library on unknown business in droves.

Mrs. Isaacsen heard the echoes of madness, I was sure, because when she handed me my mug, she said, "Maybe I should be offering you something cold. You're smoldering."

"I hate money," I said.

"I see. Any particular reason?"

"Because I need it and I have to work to get it, which doesn't give me any time to enjoy what I love or to help my friends who are worse off than I am! And I hate my job and I hate it when people who *do* have money lord it over you like you're supposed to do whatever they want and if you don't they'll try to run you down."

I hauled in a breath, but Mrs. Isaacsen only said, "Is that all of it?"

"No. I'm getting stuff from that Secret Admirer person again and I'm sick of it because all it does is confuse me even more— and I think you know what's going on with him and that makes me feel like even more of a checker."

"Oh." Mrs. Isaacsen put her mug down. "So some of this anger is directed at me."

I felt a sharp tug inside. "Not anger—just—"

"Laura, it's all right to be angry. It's what you do with it that matters." Her eyes crinkled. "But, darlin', before we go on, I have to ask you—you feel like a 'checker'?"

"I got that from Celeste," I said.

"That would account for my confusion."

"I feel like all these people are moving me around on some giant checkerboard."

"I see—the giant checkerboard of life. And the Secret Admirer is one of the players, and you think I know something about him."

"It's not that I think you've been lying to me—I just want to know how it could be that right at the same time you're asking us what material things are important to us and you're all talking about treasures, he leaves me this treasure chest in my locker with a note about storing up precious treasures, and then today it's missing and there's a note saying 'beware of thieves that will steal your treasures'."

Mrs. Isaacsen looked right into me. "First of all, Laura, let me assure you I do not know who is doing this, and I'm certainly not in cahoots with him—"

"I'm sorry—"

"Though I can see how you would think that. I'm more concerned about how this person is getting into your locker and invading your privacy."

"It's creeping me out, too. Should I even pay any attention to the notes?"

She toyed with the chain on her glasses. "Now, that is the thing, isn't it? What he's saying to you is what I've been trying to say to all of you—but maybe to you most of all: what are your priorities? Are you still surrendering to what God wants for you?"

"I thought I was! I'm sure he wants me to sing—and I've been praying about being able to get into the program here and now I have an actual part—did you know about that?"

"Celeste told me. I guess that would be the reason you missed your appointment with me after school on Friday."

There was another sharp tug. "Oh, my gosh! I got so excited, I totally forgot! I'm so sorry—"

"Understandable. And I don't think the musical is the problem. Mr. Howitch is absolutely delighted with you, by the way."

"I love him! I love the whole thing—it's like it really is a God-thing."

"I agree. Drink your tea before it gets cold."

I took a drag out of the cup and let its warmth ease into my chest. I was already feeling as if something had been lifted off my heavy pile—only it hadn't. I tightened my fingers around the mug.

"But God isn't the only one I have to surrender to," I said. I reminded her about the car situation, and the new importance that now had with the house damage Dad had to pay for.

"You do have a responsibility," Mrs. Isaacsen said. "But it's about discipline too. You have to respect your father, but you only have to surrender to God."

"Tell my dad that."

"You tell him."

"No stinkin' way!"

Mrs. Isaacsen gave one of her throaty chuckles. "Part of respecting your father is giving him the benefit of the doubt—you know, operating from the off chance that he might actually understand."

"Yeah, but you talk about discipline—he'll hand down a punishment if I even breathe disrespectfully."

She shook the crispy-gray head. "I'm talking about self-discipline, which has nothing to do with punishment. It's about focus and control. You have to discipline yourself to listen to God, to watch for Him, and to act on what He's telling you whether it scares you or not."

I looked glumly into my now lukewarm tea. "You're talking about reading my Bible—journaling—having quiet time with God." I rolled my eyes. "I still do that, only it's harder since I started working, and it's even worse now that I have this new part." I could feel the tears coming again. "Do you think God wants me to give up the musical?"

"No, I do not. I think what God wants you to do is this—" She perched the glasses on her nose and picked up a pad of paper. "I have a two-part assignment for you. Now, this Secret Admirer of yours may be something of a fruitcake, but so far he's giving you good advice. I'd rather you got it straight from the Bible, though, so here are some verses I want you to study—"

"But—when?"

"That's part two. I'd like you to try to give up anything in your life that you absolutely do not need." She peered over the tops of the half-glasses. "And that does not include the musical. That is an essential. You must develop your gift." She ripped the page from the pad and handed it to me. "Doing that is going to give you more time for this."

I couldn't read what she'd written because tears were blurring my vision.

"Do you promise?" I said.

"I've never seen it fail yet."

I stood up to go, and then I thought of something—something that brought on the hardest tug yet.

"Um, Mrs. I.?" I said. "I told Mr. Howitch that I would talk to you about giving up Group meetings until the show is over. I have so much stuff to learn—"

"I know," she said, "and I told him no. He was quite cooperative."

I was totally surprised, but tried not to show it. "I guess Group is a need, then, huh?"

"Oh, yes, darlin', it is."

But I wasn't sure that tutoring with Trent was one, not right now. It struck me as I was leaving the counseling suite that I had forgotten to mention my extra rehearsals to him.

When the bell rang, I headed off to the library, praying that Trent would already be there.

He was – and he told me there was no way I could possibly make an A in chemistry without two tutoring sessions a week. I didn't have time to argue with him. I had to get to my rehearsal with Mr. Howitch and the Pink Ladies.

Even though I didn't feel good about his reaction, I already felt lighter, as if some layers were starting to come off. It felt so right, I wanted to get rid of more—and the shoplifting issue was the one I wanted to dump first. It was definitely something I didn't need. The question was—how?

chapter eleven

"You were late, Laura," Yolanda said to me that night.

"Yes, ma'am. I was in rehearsal, and then—"

"When you sign on with us, you make an unspoken promise that your extra-curricular school activities will not encroach on your work hours."

"It won't happen again," I said. "But I do need to talk to you about a couple of things –"

"Later."

She walked away, and I started for the break room to clock in, but then she turned around suddenly and I nearly ran up her shins. "I've come to expect you to have a better work ethic than the others," she said with a penetrating look.

"Yes, ma'am," I said. I clocked in, peeled off my jacket, dumped my purse, and went out on the floor. *So much for being in favor with the queen*, I thought. *Wait 'til I tell Owen.*

But Yolanda asked Owen to stay in the back and unpack the new stock, so it looked like I was going to have to avoid Wendy on my own. But that didn't turn out to be a problem because she, too, had another focus: Gigi, Natalie, Vance, and Ethan all arrived at the beginning of the shift and loitered around the store, gathering around Wendy and whispering every chance they got—which was often. A stern-looking man in a business suit walked in, and he and Yolanda closed themselves up in Yolanda's office.

At least They didn't try to hold court in the dressing rooms, so I concentrated on not concentrating on Them. It wasn't easy. I was under their surveillance as I helped a giggly thirteen year old find a pair of jeans in size zero, and when I replaced an entire rack of socks that had been "accidentally" knocked over by one of Them. I was counting the minutes until I could go on break.

Evidently, so were They. Three times I heard Vance say to Wendy, "When can you get outta here?" The third time he asked, she about snapped his head off, which did NOT fly with His Bad Boyness. After that, the three of Them stood near the doorway with their arms folded or their hands on their hips, looking at their watches and sighing. Wendy took to gnawing at her cuticles. It was 30 seconds 'til my break whensomebody said,

"So, Laurie?"

I turned to face a smiling Wendy. The rest of the Court was gone.

"Yeah?" I said.

"Would you mind switching breaks with me? If I don't go now, my friends are going to start having puppies right out there in the mall."

She wrinkled her nose this time as she smiled. I could feel the bile rising in my throat.

I resisted the urge to attack her with a price gun and said, "Sure. Go ahead."

After all, I thought as she practically ran into the break room and came out with her purse, *all I wanted was to get away from them*. In fact, the minute they were gone, I actually had a charitable thought.

Maybe they're going to return the top and that's why they're so worked up. But the thought fell apart like the little house of cards it was. Even if they did return the top, how was I going to know they had? I didn't know anything about the one Natalie walked out with, except that it had to have come from a sale table where the merchandise didn't have security tags. They could have returned it already for all I knew—it could be sitting right there on top of a pile…Except I knew better. I just knew.

Wendy was gone longer than fifteen minutes. By minute number twenty, I really had to use the restroom, and I was literally doing the pee-pee dance as I carried a customer's load of try-ons to the dressing room attendant.

"Get back here, Wendy," I said under my breath, "or there's going to be a puddle on the floor."

No sooner were the words out of my mouth then Wendy ran in, brushing roughly against a woman with a baby on her hip. She didn't stop to apologize, but hurled her purse behind the counter, jammed a headset on, and dove for the same sock rack I had already reorganized to perfection. The Mother was still standing there, gaping in disbelief.

I was about to wet my pants, so I raced for the bathroom, grabbing my jacket on the way so I'd be ready for break. When I came out, much relieved, Yolanda was waiting for me.

"We do not haul tail through the store and plow down the customers," she said. Her voice was arctic.

"I'm sorry. I had to use the bathroom."

"Why didn't you go when you were on your break?"

"I haven't had my break."

"Laura, your break was twenty minutes ago."

"I switched with Wendy."

"Why?"

"Because she asked me to, and I didn't see—"

Yolanda narrowed her eyes at me. "Do you do everything Wendy asks you to?"

"No! I mean, no, ma'am—"

"I wouldn't advise it."

"Yes, ma'am."

I stood there, feeling an odd sensation run through me as I watched myself fall out of favor.

But Yolanda's face suddenly went slack, and she closed her eyes.

"I'm sorry, Laura," she said. "You're one of my best. I don't mean to take my stuff out on you. I'm just under a lot of pressure right now."

She smoothed a wrinkle out of my jacket sleeve and walked away.

I made sure there was change in my pocket and made a beeline for the first pay phone I could find out in the mall. As I poked out Celeste's number, my finger trembled, and I didn't even know why. Maybe my best friend could tell me.

But there was no answer—and then I started to panic. I would call Joy Beth. Even a grunt might calm the fears that were ambushing me from nowhere. But one of her half dozen brothers said, "She ain't talkin' to nobody." I felt a stab of guilt. It was like she dropped off the planet, and I hadn't had time to look for her."

But as I stopped just in front of the Gap's display window and peered between the plastic bodies wearing size-two shorts, I had to think about Them. I could see Wendy at the clearance turtlenecks, absently folding. Her eyes were on the front door, and even as I watched, she wadded up the same shirt twice—three times—and was starting on a fourth when her face lit up and she went to the door, tossing the turtleneck behind her and missing the counter completely.

"Hey," said a voice behind me.

I jumped as if I'd been shot. I could see Gigi's reflection in the window. I slowly turned to face her. *I don't have time for them. I'm not going to waste any more time on them—*

"Hey," I said back.

There was something deliberate about the usually fluid Gigi tonight. Her arms seemed almost robotic as she brushed a dark tendril of hair off her forehead and adjusted her shoulder bag. Even her facial expressions looked carefully planned and executed.

"So," she said finally, "did you talk to him?"

"Who?"

"Mr.—the music teacher."

"About what?" I said.

"Natalie."

"No," I said. My eyes felt like stones in their sockets.

"Oh," she said. She drew her brows together. "I just thought you'd have more compassion than that. You know, from what I've heard about you."

"I have compassion," I said. Of course, the moment the words left my tongue, I wanted to grab them out of the air. *I'm not going to get defensive with this chick*, I told myself. *I'm NOT going to waste my time.*

"Whatever," she said. "But I think you're going to regret it."

"Is that a threat?" That's more like it, Laura. *Keep it up.*

Gigi let her eyes slide over me like a pair of ice skates. "No," she said. "It's a guarantee." With that she skated away, leaving me cursing myself for letting her have the last word. I turned away and closed my eyes.

God—I hate this whole thing. Please—whatever I'm supposed to dump from my life, please show me what it is, okay? Focus—discipline—

control. Mrs. Isaacsen's words rose in my head, but I couldn't read between their lines. All I could remember was:

Give up everything you don't absolutely need.

And read that Bible verse—the one she'd written down for me.

As I shook myself out and went for the door, I promised myself I was going to read it the minute I got home. I needed all the help I could get.

I'm GOING to get on top of this, I told myself. *I have to.*

For the rest of my shift, I found myself praying, sometimes even moving my lips. I caught Wendy looking my way several times, watching me the way my mom watched Bonnie when she was expecting her to break out in an allergic reaction. Once I almost said, *What?* But I'd promised myself I wasn't going to waste my time on Them. I was going to keep my promise.

At closing time Owen leaned against the wall as I came out of the break room, "You ready?"

"For what?" I said.

"For me to walk you out to your car." He lifted an eyebrow, which tonight had the tiniest of gold rings in it. Yolanda must not have noticed it. "Tell me you haven't been going out in that parking lot alone."

"No stinkin' way," I said. "Thanks for waiting for me."

"I was going into withdrawal anyway. I haven't talked to you in days."

I giggled and stuck my hands into my jacket pockets as we both nodded to Yolanda when she let us out and locked the door behind us.

He tucked his arm through mine. "Where did you park?"

"Over there," I said. I pointed in the general direction of Twenty-third Street and patted my jacket pocket for my keys. No keys. I dug around in my purse until I found them and pulled them out.

Owen interrupted my thoughts. "You want to try again? I don't see the heap."

"My car isn't a heap! It's just—"

I stopped and slowly untangled myself from Owen's arm.

"What?" he said. "What's wrong?"

"Owen," I said. "My car's gone."

chapter twelve

My father arrived about the same time the Panama Beach Police did. By then I had become a hysterical mess in Owen's arms. Dad leaped from the van and ran to me without even closing the door. I cringed in anticipation.

"Laura," he said. "Are you all right?" The tremor in his voice surprised me. "I'm okay," I said. "Daddy—I'm sorry. I locked the car and every-thing—but when I came out of work, it was gone— I'm so sorry—"

"Laura, for heaven's sake," he said. His eyes actually looked bewildered. "This is not your fault, Baby Girl. It could happen to anyone."

He hadn't called me that name in a while, which was probably why a new barrage of tears came on as I fell into his hug.

"I know you're upset," Dad said into my hair. "But it's only a car. Now try to pull yourself together. The police want to ask you some questions—"

As soon as Dad got me to the place where I could speak without choking to death, he stood out in the parking lot with one officer while the other one, whose badge read STILES, ushered me into the front seat of the squad car. Just sitting there made me feel like a criminal.

"I know something like this can really shake you up," Officer Stiles said. "I just need to ask if anybody you know might be playing a joke on you."

I shook my head. "My friends would never play a joke like this."

"Do you have any enemies?"

Fortunately, Officer Stiles was jotting down some notes when I felt my face turn scarlet. He looked up.

"You haven't stolen anybody's boyfriend? Didn't take someone's place on the cheerleading squad? Nothing like that?"

I shook my head again.

Officer Stiles fished in his shirt pocket and pulled out a business card. "I'm going to let you go home now because you've had a pretty rough night. Call this number if you think of anything that might help us find your car."

"Okay," I said. I curled my damp fingers around the card and I stuck it in my jacket pocket.

Dad was still talking to the other officer when I hurried toward the van.

"You okay?"

Owen was sitting on the curb beneath a parking lot light. I sat next to him.

"Did you tell them?" he asked.

"Tell them what?"

"Who took your car."

I looked at the toes of my Skechers. "I don't know who took my car," I said.

"Just like you don't know who tried to run you down the other night."

"*I don't know,*" I said.

"Come on, Laura. Let's go over the list of grievances They have against you right now."

"This is stupid. They wouldn't steal my car over a bunch of little stuff like that."

"Just list them." Owen held up a finger. "Number one—"

I gave an exaggerated sigh. "Okay—number one: I ran into Vance's brand new truck. But I paid for it!"

"Number two?"

"I won't drop out of the musical so Natalie can come back and do her part."

"Number three?"

I grunted. "They know that *I* know Wendy helped them shoplift a top from the store. I should never have told you about that part. Now you're in a funky position because you know."

"I'm not worried." Owen pulled his pad out of his pocket. "Could Wendy have gotten to your car keys?"

"I have my keys."

"But did she have the opportunity to take them out of your purse and put them back later?"

I thought back to Wendy's hurried re-entry into the store after her break and shook my head. "She got back a few minutes late, so she went right to the front counter and started to work."

Owen looked up from his doodling. "And then you went on break, which would have given her a chance to put the keys back in your purse. You didn't take it with you, right?"

"No." I could feel my eyes widening. "They all came back just as I was coming in from *my* break, but I didn't see them with Wendy because Gigi, like, accosted me in front of the store."

"Which gave Wendy a chance to get the keys from Vance and put them back in your purse." Owen finished a stroke with a flourish of the pencil.

"I still can't prove anything," I said.

"Who says you have to? You just tell the cops what you know and *they* prove it. That's their job."

I raked my fingers through my hair, which had long since come out of its braid and was now hanging in bedraggled strings. The tears were sneaking up on me again.

"I want to do that. I really do. I'm sick of Them. I have more important—" I pressed the tips of my fingers against my eyes. "But if I share what I think I know and it turns out it wasn't Them, what then?"

"The police don't reveal their sources. Vance and Them are never going to know it was you—" He glanced at me sideways from the pad. "Unless you keep walking around with that guilty look on your face. Anyway, once the cops nail them, you won't have to worry about Them anymore."

I shook my head hard. "I don't have to worry about Them now! They've already done the worst thing They can do to me. Without my car, I can't get to work, and if I can't get to work, I can't pay back my father."

Owen was shaking his head.

"What?" I said.

"You crossed them on the Natalie thing. They know you know Wendy and her Ladyships ripped off a shirt, and they know they can scare you. So naturally they expect you to cave in over this— drop out of the show, promise to drop the shoplifting deal, whatever. But you're not going to do that, right?"

"No, I'm not." I tried to straighten my shoulders.

"Okay – cool. But if you don't at least tell the police that Vance and Them have a motive to hurt you, then don't think They won't stoop even lower than this. Besides, it's not just about you. Unless somebody stops them, they'll keep doing this same kind of thing to other people."

I sagged again. "Why did you have to say that?"

"Because it's true. And because I knew it would get to you." Owen slung an arm around my shoulders. "You're too good a person to let them get away with this."

I turned to look at him. Our noses were almost touching. "You're the one who told me to look the other way when I saw stuff like this. Now you're telling me to do the exact opposite."

Suddenly Owen wouldn't look at me. He turned his attention to the doodles on his notepad. "I've changed my whole attitude about that."

"Because—"

I could almost hear him swallow. "Because of you," he said.

The next morning I was sure I had more anxiety than blood running in my veins. Mom ironed a blouse for me, packed a lunch so big it could feed Celeste's entire stable of males, and insisted on driving me to school instead of making me take the bus. But all of her kind gestures did nothing to calm me down.

At school the locker hallway was filled with kids and noise, but that faded when I pulled open my locker door and the off-white parchment envelope slid out.

I went cold.

His last note had said, *Beware of thieves who will steal your treasure.*

The warning was now so clear it frightened me. I fought the rising compulsion not to open the envelope, until a thought struck me: *He could be trying to tell me what to do next.*

After all, that message had been a hint that I was about to be robbed, and—bingo!—there went my car. If I went back and read his other notes, I might find more clues. I tore into it.

Don't be afraid. You are as rich as the birds of the air.

Your Secret Admirer

My spine sagged into a disappointed curve. *Wonderful. I have Mrs. Isaacsen telling me to give up everything I don't absolutely need, and he's telling me I'm rich!*

By the time I got to second period, I was so tired of people asking me if it was true that my Volvo had been chopped up for parts or that I had been car-jacked, I was considering asking the sub for a restroom pass so I could go hide in a stall. Then somebody pulled a desk next to mine, and a smooth brownish hand reached over to my desktop.

"Hey," Stevie said. "Sorry to hear about your car."

At first I could only stare into the face that looked innocently back at me, her creamy brow puckered in concern. *What an actress!* I thought *You really ought to audition for The Glass Menagerie.* And then the anger started to rise. I gripped the sides of my history book so I wouldn't break her nose with it.

"It was stolen," I said coldly. "Somebody just took it out of the mall parking lot while I was at work." In my head I added, *As if you didn't know.*

Stevie was nodding solemnly. "That must have totally freaked you out. It's like you've been violated when somebody steals from you."

It was impossible to do anything but stare at this girl whose friends were probably responsible for my missing Volvo.

"Look," Stevie said, "I know we hardly know each other—"

We don't know each other at ALL. I don't WANT to know you!

"But you just look SO bummed out, and trust me, I know what that feels like."

"Really," I said. My voice sounded as flat as a dial tone.

"We lost a lot in the storm. One of our boats was wrecked — our whole downstairs was under three feet of water, and then my dad broke his leg when he fell off the roof trying to fix it. It was the first time I ever thought about losing him. I guess you don't think about stuff like that until something bad happens."

"No, I guess not," was all I could say.

I was too busy looking for cracks in the empathy-veneer. There weren't any.

"Well, anyway—" Stevie removed her hand from my desk and

nervously pulled a megaphone charm back and forth on the silver chain around her neck. She almost looked uncertain. "If you ever need somebody to talk to, I've seen you with your friends and I know you probably have plenty of support—but if you want to talk to someone who's been there—" Her voice trailed off as she shrugged.

"Sure," I said woodenly. "Thanks."

What just happened? I said to myself. *What the HECK just happened?*

At the end of class, I raced to Mrs. Isaacsen's office so I could get there before the rest of the Group.

"You're an early bird," she started to say, and then she really looked at me. "Laura, what on earth is wrong, darlin'?"

"You know how you told me to give up everything I don't absolutely need?" I said. "Well—the one thing I thought I DID need got taken from me. You think God's doing that?"

Mrs. Isaacsen pointed to a chair. "Why don't you sit down and tell me what in the world you're talking about?"

I didn't even have my buns all the way on the seat before I had most of the story out. Her eyes got larger with every word. When I was done, she said, "Well, bless your heart."

I glanced back at the door, but nobody had shown yet. "Do you think God was trying to tell me I didn't really need the car?" *Please, please tell me you think it was,* I wanted to cry out to her. *Then I'll know it wasn't Them. God wouldn't use Them…*

But Mrs. Isaacsen was shaking her head. "You've said it your-self—we don't think God makes things like that happen."

"Oh," I said. "I guess maybe it's just a start in giving up what I don't need." I flashed her a smile that I hoped disguised my anxiety. "I think I'll clean out my closet tonight."

She didn't answer at first, a sure sign she wasn't buying my cover-up. "The things you don't need aren't necessarily material things. When you give up all of the real baggage in your life, what you're left with are the sacred gifts of God. That's when you're really rich."

I jerked in the chair.

"You know, having something stolen from you feels an awful lot like you've been personally violated," she went on. " It could take you a while to get past that part—"

"Who got violated?" said K.J. as she sailed in. She peered at me. "Did they, like, rape you or something when they took your car?"

"Rape?" Celeste said. From the doorway, she scanned the room in sheer horror. "Who got raped?"

While Mrs. Isaacsen got all of that sorted out, I sat back in the chair and tried not to freak out. The most unsettling thing for me was the fact that Stevie had said almost exactly the same words to me as Mrs. Isaacsen just did. And then Mrs. I. said I was close to being really "rich"—like in the Secret Admirer's latest note.

Celeste leaned close to my ear. "Why didn't you tell me?" she said. "For the last two hours, I've heard you were kidnapped, that you were thrown out on the side of the road, that your family was held hostage—I've been goin' bonkers!"

"It was too late to call you last night," I said. "Honest, Celeste— I've been dying to talk to you, AND—" I looked over at an empty chair. "Where's Joy Beth?"

"I don't KNOW!" Celeste let her hands drop to her thighs, clad in a pair of plaid crop pants reminiscent of the fifties. "Between the two of you, I'm going to need some Valium soon."

The door opened enough for a head to pop in. I recognized one of the tidy little secretaries from the main office.

"I'm just making a delivery. Is Laura Duffy in here?"

I jolted upright in the chair and raised my hand. Visions of subpoenas—arrest warrants for lying to a police officer—hate letters with words cut from magazines—spun in my head.

But as the door opened wider, I saw she was holding a bird-cage with two very plump mourning doves inside. The room filled up with *Oh's* and *Ah's* and a "Look how cute!"

"It's got a note on it," K.J. said. "Read it out loud."

"I think we need to observe some boundaries here," Mrs. Isaacsen said to her.

I was still gazing, open-mouthed, at the parchment envelope, when the office lady said, "Just so you know, students are not supposed to receive deliveries like flowers—and birds—here at school. You need to tell that to whoever sent you this."

"Yes, ma'am," I said.

"Who sent it?" K.J. said.

I looked up at Mrs. Isaacsen.

"I think Laura needs a little privacy," she said. "It's a gorgeous-day. Girls, let's go out on the lawn. You can catch up with us when ever you're ready, Laura." I wanted to hug her. I knew the gift was from my Secret Admirer. And as usual, I couldn't ignore him. Whoever this person was, he was the most compelling human being I had ever not known. When the Group was gone, I picked up the envelope and held my breath as I read the words inside the note:

Set them free. They'll be taken care of.

So will you, Sweet Girl. Set yourself free, too.

Your Secret Admirer

I laid my head against the bars of the cage and cried.

chapter thirteen

I met Celeste at the cafeteria door when the bell rang, with the birdcage in hand.

"You gonna tell me what's going on, Duffy?" Celeste said. "I'm going bananas, here! Are you okay?" "I guess so—" " She gave a nod toward the befuddled doves, "What about THIS? That envelope's just like the one that fell out of your locker when you got that treasure chest thing—don't think I didn't see that—so, come on, is this from that one guy?"

"My 'Secret Admirer'? Yeah."

"That chest thing, too?"

"Yeah—which is now missing from my locker."

"You mean, like stolen?"

"Well, it was never really mine to begin with, but—"

"I don't want to sound like K.J, but what does the message say?"

"It says I should set these birds free and they'll be all right, just like I'll be all right if I set myself free."

Celeste twisted to gaze full on at the birdcage. "Well, how cool is that?" she said. "So—are you gonna do it?"

"Well—"

"If that's what the message says, then it seems like you should do it."

I tried not to stare at her. Of all the reactions I expected, 'Just do what the message says,' wasn't on the list.

"You don't think it's weird?" I said.

"Of course I think it's weird. It IS weird." Celeste shrugged her shoulders, her eyes shining. "But what's wrong with weird?"

"Then you're gonna help me, right?" I said. "You're not gonna make me be weird by myself?"

"No, Duffy, since you're my best friend and you're about to do something that could potentially change your life, I think I'll just go off and buy myself a hamburger. Are you kidding me? Grab the birds. I've got the perfect place."

We jumped into the Mercedes and headed down Magnolia Avenue.

"You ever been to McKenzie Park?" she said.

"No."

"You gotta get out more, Duffy."

"You really think this could change my life—letting these birds go?" I said.

Celeste nodded. "To me it's like you've been singled out by some-body for something important. I don't think this Secret Admirer guy is just interested in a hot date."

"Gee, thanks."

"Get over it, Duffy. I'm sure the dude thinks you're hot, but I think this is *beyond* hot." She pulled the Mercedes into a park-ing place.

I felt as if I were being pulled by a silk rope, and although I didn't know where it was taking me, I wanted to go.

Celeste led me across the park, past some ancient trees. It had to be the quietest place in Panama Beach, for one thing. Yes, there were sounds—sunlit streams of water splashing softly into a round brick fountain, a train whistling in the Somewhere, a car swishing past, and church bells ringing from some buildings to our right. The hush begged me to join it.

"This is beautiful," I whispered to Celeste. It was an oasis right in the middle of my misery.

Along the path date palms sprouted up here and there, waving their fronds like they were calling our attention to things, and around the square gazebo at the end of one of the pathways, azalea bushes were ripe with buds waiting to pop.

"They have concerts and stuff here," Celeste said. "I can totally imagine you up there singing."

My imagination had beaten her there. "Me too," I said.

We headed for a bench that sat in a splash of light beside the walkway, as if the sun had chosen the spot for us. With cage in hand, Celeste turned to me.

"Perfect?" she said.

"Perfect," I said.

We both just stood there. I let the breeze brush against my skin, the sun release the tension in my muscles. It was as close as I had felt to God in a long time.

"It's like we're praying," Celeste whispered. "Only we're not saying anything."

Celeste had her eyes closed and her face turned upward. The sun was spinning gold in her hair. She was more beautiful than I had ever seen her.

"I don't think we have to say anything," I whispered back. "I think we're in the Presence."

I was suddenly aware of a symphony going on around us. The birds outside the cage seemed to be delighted with the day.

"I bet they're talking to our doves," I said.

"What do you think they're saying?" Celeste whispered toward the trees.

"I think they're saying, 'Come out!'"

"Yeah—like, 'What's with the cage? Dude—take some risks.'"

I grinned and lifted the latch on the cage door. For the first time, I noticed tiny pearls lined the shiny bars as if they formed the crown of an infant princess.

"Fly, little birds," I whispered. "I'm setting you free. God will take care of you."

Almost as if they'd been waiting for permission, the birds were suddenly out of the cage.

They hopped to the door and sailed up into a live oak, which held its branches out to them like open arms. The rest of the birds fell silent.

They think it's a holy moment, too, I thought. Now the doves have everything—

I gasped.

"What?" Celeste said.

"They're rich now, just like the note said."

* * * * * *

At rehearsal that afternoon, we did a run-through of act one, and I did my part off-book. When Mr. Howitch gave us our first break, he called me over to his stool.

"You're doing an excellent job, Laura. This could have been very tough on the cast, having a change at this late date, but you're handling it like a trooper. I think they all see we're going to be fine. Better than fine."

I knew I was blushing. I could practically see the heat from my face reflecting on his. "Thanks," I said. "Just—well—thanks—that's really nice of you— " He was looking at me, amused, and then he was suddenly distracted. *Okay, time for me to go,* I thought. *Before I fall all over myself.* But I couldn't help but follow his gaze to the back of the theatre.

My heart seized up like a stuck motor. Natalie was slouched in a seat with a bunch of Kleenex wadded up in each hand. Her eyes were practically swollen shut.

I chose that moment to escape backstage. Wherever Natalie was, could They be far behind?

I'm not free yet, I thought. *I'm going to be, though, right God?*

chapter fourteen

Halfway through dinner that night, I got a phone call from Celeste.

"It's an emergency. I've got info on Them. I'll be right over!"

She must have called from our driveway because it wasn't a minute later when she rang the doorbell. She refused Mom's invitation to dinner but accepted dessert. Mom sent Celeste and me back to my room with half a chocolate-raspberry torte and two forks.

"Okay," I said. "Dish."

"All right—I called up my friend Butchie Neville—you don't know him—he goes to VoTech—and I asked him how much you had to know about cars if you were going to hotwire a Volvo. I didn't ask my dad about it because he'd want to know why I wanted to know about hotwiring and before I knew it, I'd be in a convent or something. Anyway, Butchie said you had to know 'a lot,' and if you weren't a gear head or a professional grand-theft-auto type, it could take you a while to do it." Celeste took a much-needed breath. "So if Vance and Ethan *did* take the car, they probably didn't hotwire it because they never even pump their own gas." "But it could have been some pro."

"Not necessarily. I also talked to one of my dad's pit crew guys who did time for running a chop shop—and who's NOT gonna tell my dad I talked to him about this because my dad doesn't know he has a criminal record. Anyway he said a pro would only steal an older car to sell the parts, and Volvo parts aren't bringing in the big bucks right now."

I breathed for her, since she looked as if she were going to go on until she passed out.

"Not only that, but it was taken from a public parking lot, right under those big ol' honkin' lights. Carb told me a pro's probably gonna play it safer than that unless he wants a thrill."

"His name's Carb? Like carbohydrate?" I said.

"No, *Carburetor*. Now try to focus, would ya, Duffy? There's more."

I hoped so. So far, none of this was all that conclusive. They always called it "circumstantial evidence" on *Law and Order*. I needed some DNA matches or something.

Celeste rearranged herself on the bed, completely ignoring the torte that threatened to topple over on its side and dump raspberry juice all over my bedspread.

"So what else ya got?" I said.

"I gotta hold of Justin Hartman—captain of the basketball team. I went out with him once but he kept pawing me so I slapped him and now he respects me. Anyway, he hangs out with Vance and that crowd sometimes."

"And—" I said.

"Okay, so I got him talking about stuff Vance and Them have done in the past. I gotta tell you, I was so slick getting this stuff out of him. It was almost too easy, you know what I'm saying?"

"Easier than I'm getting it out of you!" My voice was teetering on the edge of total exasperation.

"I wanted you to have the background—"

"Cel-E-este!"

"Anyhow, he starts telling me about how they have this process for getting what they want. They do it with their parents, even, and they brag about how it works. He said first they just expect to get what they want, so usually they do. Y'know—the money, the looks, the sexy charm thing, all that pretty much guarantees it as far as they're concerned. If that doesn't automatically work, then they have enough nerve to just go to the person who has what they want and tell that person to give it to them."

"Like Gigi telling me to give the part back to Natalie."

"Yeah. Or they just take whatever it is. And sometimes they'll out-and-out use somebody to help them do it—without even trying to hide it or anything."

"Wendy and the shoplifting thing."

"Right. And then, if *that* doesn't get them there or if somebody gets suspicious, they issue a warning—like a nasty warning. Now here's where it gets good." As if on cue, we both leaned in like we had to keep it from the very walls themselves.

"Justin told me that one time this girl told a teacher that some kids—she didn't say who, but she was talking about Them—got their term papers off the Internet. The teacher was going to make everybody in the class write a whole different paper IN CLASS for the same number of points. So, let's see, it was Gigi and Ethan and Vance and some other kids in their group who weren't in the class, they found out who the girl was and got themselves invited to a party at her house. Then they handed her computer out her bedroom window to the term paper cheats—during the party!"

"No stinkin' way!"

"Hey, Justin knows because they asked him to do it with them and he told them he wasn't allowed to go to the party, which was a lie, he just didn't want to say he thought they were wrong. He can be kind of a wimp sometimes."

"Which is why he didn't turn them in."

"Nobody even pointed a finger at them. After the party, that girl went to her teacher and said she'd been wrong about the Internet thing and then the computer miraculously turned up on her front porch in the middle of the night. I guess the girl figured it wasn't hurting HER if they cheated, so she totally dropped it."

I leaned back against my pillows, staring at the ceiling.

"What?" Celeste said.

"So what you're trying to say is that if either Term Paper Girl or Justin had had the guts to report what happened, then They'd all be living in Juvie right now and maybe my car wouldn't have been stolen."

She didn't answer.

"That's what you're saying isn't it?" I said. "That I need to tell the police what I know, to protect other people."

"Yes and no. See, Justin told me that if a warning like that doesn't work, they'll go farther. They have second and third stringers in this group, y'know—people who want to be in with them so bad, they'll work for them on the outside if They do get suspended or whatever—which hardly ever happens because their parents think they own the school, the school BOARD."

I sat up again. "How much farther will they go?"

"Justin said when the coach made some other kid first string quarterback instead of Vance's older brother last year, they put something in the quarterback's Gatorade and he passed out in the middle of the game!"

"And nobody told?"

"No. If anybody else knew about it, they didn't want to be the next victim."

"Including Justin."

"Justin says it isn't his responsibility to teach them right from wrong."

I sagged from the top down. "So even if he knew that Vance stole my car, he wouldn't testify to it?"

Celeste's lips eased into a smug smile. "We don't need him. He let slip with one little detail he wasn't even aware of."

"So tell me!"

"Okay, I'm all going off on him about being a coward and a wienie and he goes, 'Hey, you know what—if I was going to go forward with what I know, the only person who could convince me to do it would be Stevie'."

"Stevie?"

"Yeah. He was just saying it to try to make me jealous—like I WOULD be—but I caught on and I started just going with it. I go, 'Why her?' and he goes, 'Because she doesn't want to be part of them anymore, only it's kind of like the Mafia. She's afraid to bail because she knows too much.'"

I shivered. "It can't be that bad—can it?"

"They drugged somebody's sports beverage! And I haven't even told you the worst one. When some chick they didn't like got on the cheerleading squad, they planted a bag of pot in her locker. She went DOWN for that. Anyway, according to Justin, that marijuana frame-up was the thing that got Stevie thinking she didn't want to be a part of them anymore."

"So she wasn't putting on an act, after all."

"What are you talking about?"

I told her about the scene with Stevie in history.

Celeste was nodding soberly. "Maybe she really is trying to clean up her act."

"She said something that made actual sense, and then Mrs. Isaacsen said it again almost right after that in group. She said you feel like you've been violated when you lose something that's really important to you. You know what's really scaring me?" I said.

"About eighty things, I bet! This is huge."

"I think I actually get why They just keep pushing and pushing for what they want—because when they don't get it, they feel like it's a violation of their rights."

"It's not!"

"But THEY think it is." I got up and paced. "I wish I could talk to Mrs. I. right now. I can always figure things out when I'm talking to her—"

"Don't you think we should get back to figuring out what you're gonna do about your car?"

"I think that's what I'm doing."

"So what do you want to do—call Mrs. I. on the phone?"

"No!"

"Okay, then think about what she did say to you the last time you guys talked. And sit down, would you, Duffy? You're making me nauseous."

I started to perch on the edge of the bed, but I sprang up again. "The Bible verses!" I blurted.

"What Bible verses?"

"I haven't even looked at them yet!"

"Why can't you ever answer a question directly?" Celeste said.

"The answers are always there! What did I do with that piece of paper?"

I lunged for the pile on the chair, tossing items of clothing behind me like a dog digging a hole.

"What are you doing?"

"Checking pockets."

"Then check your jacket. You always look like a pregnant kangaroo with that thing on."

I snatched up my jacket and pulled out two fists full of assorted scraps, including cough drop wrappers and the paper off a tampon.

"That should be helpful," Celeste said dryly. She crawled over to where I was sitting on the bed and spread the mess out on the bedspread. "Here's that cop's card. That could come in handy—"

"Here it is—," I said. "Could you get me my—"

But Celeste was already presenting me with my Bible, which

had been lying on the floor near the foot of the bed with its pages
splayed open. She took the paper out of my hand.

"I'll give you the verse, you look it up."

"Go."

"Matthew 6:19-21."

I flipped through the pages, thin as onion skin, until I found it.
My eyes started to skim.

"Read it out loud," Celeste said.

"Uh—okay," I said. "Here we go: 'Do not store up for yourselves
treasures on earth, where moth and rust destroy, and where thieves
break in and steal. But store up for yourselves treasures in heaven,
where moth and rust do not destroy, and where thieves do not
break in and steal. For where your treasure is, there your heart will
be also'."

Celeste drew in her brows. "Well, of course nobody can steal your
stuff if it's in heaven. How are they gonna get to it?"

"I think that's the point. If it's the kind of stuff that matters in
heaven, it can't BE stolen."

"So God doesn't care about your car."

"I'm sure He doesn't—and neither do I! I don't care if I ever see it
again. Maybe God's trying to tell me to just forget about it. I wish
He'd tell my father that."

"YOU oughta tell your father that."

"Mrs. Isaacsen said that, too—like he ever listens to me. He's too
busy playing the big protector."

"It's in the father contract, Duffy. But you're getting off the
subject. If the Bible is saying—"

"It's Jesus saying it."

"Okay, so if Jesus is saying that what really matters is what
matters to Him, then that's what you have to take care of."

"Yeah."

"I wanna know who's gonna take care of the other stuff, then,
you know, like—food, a roof over your head—" She grunted.
"The little things."

"What's the other verse?"

Celeste consulted the paper. "Matthew 6:25-34."

I ran my finger down the page. "Therefore I tell you, do not
worry about your life, what you will eat or drink; or about your
body, what you will wear. Is not life more important than food, and
the body more important than clothes? Look at the birds of the air;
they do not—"

"Stop."

"What?"

"Is this not freaking you out? Birds? Hello—two birds in a cage, delivered to you at school—"

"I know. It always freaks me out that every time I get a note from the Secret Admirer, it almost exactly matches the Bible verses Mrs. Isaacsen gives me."

"You don't think she—"

"No. She says she doesn't know who it is. She keeps asking me if I'm scared somebody's stalking me."

Celeste sat straight up. "Whatever's going on, Duffy," she said, "I think you have to listen to it and do what it says, or you're gonna be in big trouble."

We sat there staring at each other for what I know was a full minute. In that kind of silence and intensity, a minute is a long time. When I did speak, I had to whisper.

"You really think that?" I said.

"Don't you? I mean, you got Jesus telling you, and then Mrs. Isaacsen and this Secret Admirer guy are backing Him up—and without each other knowing it. Plus, what happened to us when we let those birds out of the cage." Celeste leaned close to me, almost grazing the cake with her chest. "I don't know about you, but I've been feeling different ever since then—I don't know, like I don't have to sweat the small stuff or *anything*."

"So maybe I don't have to sweat my car being stolen."

She sat back. "You're not saying just let this go?"

"If God doesn't care about my car—why should I? It's gonna get rusty. It definitely got stolen, so being rusty is probably the least of its problems right now." I gave a long sigh. "But—what *does* He want me to care about, then? It's obvious I'm supposed to do something or this wouldn't all feel so—REAL."

"Okay, so let's analyze." Celeste pulled back on her pinky finger. "He cares about you. He cares about you having guts. I'm sure He definitely doesn't want you to be like Justin."

I looked at her as the idea formed itself into words I couldn't have thought of on my own: "And He cares about Them."

"Meaning..."

"He loves everybody, even if they don't love Him back, so He must care about Them getting some guts, too."

"At least in Stevie's case. I don't know about the rest of Them, Duff."

"He's God. He doesn't think like we do."

"So what do you think He's thinking?"

Then it came to me. It was so much easier when I was talking it out with somebody.

"If I'm God and I care about everybody, then I want everybody to feel free. So—He probably wants Them to be free from the whole I'm-so-violated thing all the time. If they knew what was really important, they wouldn't be grabbing for all this other stuff."

Celeste pointed her eyes at me. "I don't know if you can teach them that, Duffy. I told you once before, don't go preaching to them—"

"I'm not gonna do that. But I think God wants me to do something—"

"Like tell the cops what you know so they finally have to take responsibility for something—and then maybe they'll turn around." Celeste said.

"Maybe. I've gotta pray about it, though. I really have to do this right."

Celeste tapped the open Bible with her fingertip. "Didn't this just say to leave the details up to Him?"

"Yeah," I said. "But I think that means He'll give them to me. I have to wait for Him to tell me what they are—somehow."

"Wow."

"What?" I said.

"So, do you, like, just hear God talking to you all the time?"

"I wish! If I heard Him talking to me all the time, I'd never mess up like I do constantly. I guess if I were paying attention more, I'd hear Him more."

"But then He makes you pay attention. I mean, how are you supposed to ignore doves in a cage?"

"I guess I'm getting, like, hints all the time. I've got the Bible. I've got Mrs. I." I cocked my head at her. "I bet I even get stuff from God through you."

"Like I'm so positive God's voice is coming out of my mouth!" Celeste rolled her eyes.

"What about tonight? You brought me all this information. You're making me look at everything and make a decision. You're the one who said I need to do something because of the birdcage and the Bible verses—or I was gonna be in trouble!"

"I don't know how I know that. I just do."

"Okay, so that's God, I think."

Celeste was up on her knees at this point. "So that's how God talks to you—you just suddenly know something's right."

"Sometimes," I said.

I didn't meet her gaze, and she nailed me.

"What else?" she said. "You're holding back on me, Duffy. C'mon."

"You're gonna think I'm a psycho."

"Would you knock that off? I don't care if you're a freakin' basket case! This is real stuff, Duffy. I can feel it. And I want to know it."

She reached across the cake and grabbed my hands and squeezed them, hard. I clung back.

"I've never told anybody this before, except Mrs. Isaacsen."

"If you don't trust me by now, Duffy—"

"I do trust you. But, see, it's really hard to tell anybody that you hear a Voice whispering into your thoughts. They lock people up for that."

Celeste shook her head. "Only if the Voice is telling them to do something like murder somebody. I saw that on *E.R.*"

"No, this is a good Voice. And the thing is—I know it's God."

"Then you know what, Duffy?" she said and gave my hands another squeeze. "That's good enough for me." She scooted back then and looked down at the torte, which had survived a number of dives across it. "So, do whatever you have to do to find out what it is God wants you to do next. And then whatever it is, I'm so there."

"But don't go yet," I said. "We have to eat this cake or Mom will think we hated it and she'll need electric shock therapy or something."

"I wasn't planning on letting it go to waste." Celeste picked up one of the forks and dragged it through a layer of raspberries. "And besides, I'm not leaving until you tell me about this Owen dude." The raspberries disappeared between her lips and she looked at me through her eyelashes. "Start with when you became this Boy Magnet. I mean, not that you haven't always had the potential, but it's like all of a sudden these guys are coming out of the freakin' woodwork."

"Owen's just a friend I work with."

"Uh-huh." Celeste chewed knowingly.

"He's like a big brother. One night out in the mall parking lot— there were some guys out joy-riding—" I told her the whole thing.

She abandoned the cake again and shoved the dish aside. "So—?"

"It's another weird thing—this guy with a ponytail showed up out of nowhere and yanked me out of the way just in time. But I was the only one who saw him."

"Guy with a ponytail." Celeste stared for a minute, but I knew she wasn't really looking at me. It was as if she were asking her brain to call up something from an old file. "Wasn't it a guy with a ponytail that Joy Beth said—when was it—back in December—?"

"I've thought of that," I said. "And he was also there when that thing went down with Trent in November, only Trent said he didn't know any guy with a ponytail. See? It's too weird."

"You said God shows you stuff in a lot of different ways. I mean, if He'll send you two birds, why would he stop short of sending you a gorgeous guy?"

"And I thought *I* had an over-active imagination. Do you want to hear about Owen or not?"

Although I could tell Ponytail Boy was suddenly more intriguing, she nodded and poked absently at the cake. "Go on," she said.

"He's kind of like you, you know? He knows when I've got something on my mind and he makes me talk about it. He has this idea that the guys who almost ran me over were Vance and Ethan."

"Did you say they were in a Jeep?"

"Yeah."

"Hel-lo-o! Don't you remember the day you hit Vance's truck? Ethan was there in his Jeep. He almost rear-ended YOU, if I remember right."

"A lot of people have Jeeps."

"Well you obviously saw the guy with his head sticking out. Was it Vance?"

"Okay—this really IS psycho—he was all distorted to me— only when I described that to Owen he drew what he said I probably really saw and it was, like, the spitting image of Vance. Owen's a really good artist."

"No stinkin' way!"

"Yeah, he is. In fact, he gave me one of his sketches last night and I forgot to even look at it—it should be here in this pile some-place—"

"I'm not talking about that, I'm talking about him drawing a picture of Vance from your description."

"Yeah. It was freaky-weird." I extracted a folded piece of paper from the jumble. "Okay, here we go. He was just sitting there on the curb doodling so I don't know—"

I stopped—both my eyes and my thoughts froze as I stared at the drawing.

"So what is it?" Celeste said.

"You tell me," I said.

Celeste took the paper from me, and I watched as she studied it for only a moment before the recognition flickered in her eyes. "Dude," she said. "This is totally Wendy. And, Duffy, her hand is SO inside your jacket pocket."

"Okay, so I'm not imagining it."

"How 'bout no! It's like a photograph almost." Her eyes doubled in size as she looked up at me. "Do you think he actually saw her take the keys out of your pocket?"

"No way. He would have said so when we were talking. I think this is just how he imagined it happening."

Celeste studied the drawing again. "Did you have your keys in your pocket or your purse last night?"

"I had them in my jacket when I got to work. But when I walked out of the mall with Owen, I took them out of my—"

I could feel my mouth dropping open, as if the hinges of my jaw had suddenly given way.

"Out of my purse," I said.

"So why would he 'imagine' them coming out of your jacket when he only SAW you take them out of your purse."

"Maybe I didn't put them in my jacket when I got to work. Maybe I'm wrong—"

"Duffy—you always put everything in your jacket pockets. I told you, you look like Kanga carrying Little Roo."

"Then somebody moved them!"

"Yeah, that Wendy, she's pretty sharp, isn't she? What did she do, forget where she got them from?"

I shook my head. "I put on my jacket when I went out to break to try to call you, because I had change in my pocket. So if she took them before *she* went on break, she had to put them back in my purse."

We stared at each other again.

"Wow," Celeste said.

"But why didn't Owen just tell me that?"

"Who the heck knows? Why do boys do any of the things they do? The thing is, you KNOW now, Duffy." She got up abruptly and picked up her sweater. "I'm gonna go so you can start praying— because you've got to get moving on this fast." She looked at me hard. "And you have to, Duffy. You *have* to."

chapterfifteen

W hen Celeste left, I did my homework, and I prayed. I prayed until my chest felt warm. Then I polished off the rest of the cake and read the Bible verses over and over. Something jumped out at me that had kept quiet before. Something clear.

Where moth and rust destroy.

How did I miss that? I thought. *I got rust all over my hand that one day when I moved the treasure chest. And moths—hello! One flew right out at me!*

I waited for the creepy-chills to come over me, but they didn't. Celeste was right: this was real. And it was all pulling me by that silk rope again, just the way it had when we'd gone to the park to set the birds free. I hadn't known what I was going to do in the next second or minute, and yet what we had done by yielding to that pull had led us to where I was now—very sure that I had to go to the police with what I knew or I was going to be in a cage forever.

As I lay in bed that night with the moonlight stretching across my ceiling like silver velvet, I listened. There was no Voice, no whisper in my thoughts. But I knew I could follow the silken pull and all the details I wanted would come to me right when I needed each one. My first step, of course, was to tell my parents that I was going to the police.

Dad had already left for work when I got up the next morning, which was okay. I knew it was better to start with Mom, who would probably NOT immediately pelt me with questions about why I didn't tell the police all this stuff in the first place—*You don't fool around with the law, Laura—et cetera—et cetera—* à la Dad. I threw on my clothes, put my hair in a ponytail, and only brushed about half my teeth. I wanted to talk to Mom before Bonnie got up.

She was sitting at the kitchen table reading the paper and sipping her coffee. It struck me that I seldom saw her when she wasn't busy accomplishing something. Even when she was watching television, she was making a quilt or working on a scrapbook.

"You're up early, hon," she said. "Everything all right?"

"I need to talk to you," I said.

"You want some toast?"

She started to get up, but I sat down catty-corner from her and shook my head.

"I've been doing a lot of thinking, and I know who might have taken my car. The policeman I talked to the other night said to call him if I thought of anything, so I'm going to. I just wanted to tell you."

"Good grief," Mom said. "Are you sure, Laura? That's a pretty serious accusation."

I arranged my tone very carefully. "I'm not accusing," I said. "I'm just going to give them some information."

"What kind of information?"

I gave her the barest of details, ending with, "So—I want to call the police this morning. The officer gave me his card."

Mom scraped her chair back. "I'm going to call your father. I think maybe he should go down there and—"

"Mom, I can do this. I have to do this."

"This is the police we're talking about here, Laura." Her voice was trembling. "I don't feel comfortable about doing this without at least letting your father know."

I swallowed hard. "Then let me call him," I said.

Dad's reaction made Mom's sound like, "Sure, Laura, do whatever you want."

"You just better be very sure about this, Laura," he said after I told him the keys story for what now seemed like the hundredth time. "Don't be leading the police off on some wild goose chase."

Thank you, Dad, for that vote of confidence.

"I've prayed about this, Dad," I said. "And now I'm sure that this is what I'm supposed to do."

"That's all well and good," Dad said. "But I don't think the police will be interested in hearing what you prayed about."

"Dad—" I stopped and smoothed down my tone. "I prayed so I'd be sure I was doing the right thing. But the facts are right there in front of me. I'm just going to give the police the facts. That officer gave me his card and told me to call him."

There was a silence so long I thought for a minute we'd been cut off. It gave me a chance to close my eyes—and pretty much beg God to help me not scream into the receiver.

"All right," Dad said finally. His voice was weary. "When I get off work this afternoon, you and I will go down to the police station."

"I want to call them this morning," I said. "I'm ready."

"I think I should be with you."

"I can do this, Dad."

A sigh came through that spoke volumes. Dad had a rope too, and he was coming to the end of it. But I couldn't do anything about that. My rope was the silky one, and it was pulling me forward.

"All right," Dad said. "You call and set it up for this after-noon. I'll get off early and pick you up after school."

"After rehearsal."

"Do you want to do this or not?"

The rope was getting a few knots in it.

"I can't miss rehearsal."

"What time is it over?"

"Four o'clock."

Another sigh, this one snapping off before its natural end. "All right—I'll pick you up right at four. And in the meantime, really think about this, Laura. I want you to tell the truth, but only the truth. I know how emotions can muddy things up sometimes."

Yeah, I thought as I hung up the phone. *I'm so mad right now, I'm muddied up enough to smack somebody!*

Mom turned from the sink. "What did he say?"

"You know what he said? He said I'm a ditzy teenager who

doesn't know the truth from her own feelings, which are evidently not very reliable. And he said he doesn't trust me enough to talk to the police by myself because he's afraid I might start blubbering a bunch of female emotional stuff —AND he said he's not sure I really want to get my car back since I won't skip a required rehearsal to go the police when HE wants to go instead of just calling them right now and telling them like I wanted to do in the first place!"

Mom was shaking her head. "Your father did NOT say that." "Not in so many words—but it was all there between the lines." I jabbed my hand into my pocket, pulled out Officer Stiles' card, and went for the phone. Mom dried her hands on the dishtowel and went to get Bonnie up. Before I punched in the last number, I put my head against the wall and breathed one more prayer—and then I went for it. "Panama Beach Police." For an instant I considered hanging up. Mom and Dad were right—this was the POLICE— But the silken rope gave a gentle tug. "May I speak to Officer Stiles, please?" "He's not in. How can I help you?" "Well—my car was stolen two nights ago, and he told me if I had any more information I should call him, so I wanted to—" "Hold on—let me connect you to somebody who can help you— hold on." "But I just wanted to—" There was a brief silence, and then a woman's voice said,

"Detective Lee. This is about your stolen car??" I hesitated. *Detective?*" Officer Stiles told me to call him if I thought of anything else that might help." "What's your name, honey?" "Laura Duffy. My father just wants me to—" "Did you call last night?" "No. All I need to do is set up a time to come in and talk to Officer Stiles. My dad wants to come with me—"

"Laura, do you mind if I tape our conversation?"

"No," I said. I decided to sit down.

"Officer Stiles is a nice guy, isn't he?" the detective said.

That question surprised me, but it also let me sink into the chair.

"He is," I said. "And I'm a nice guy, too," she said with a chuckle. "I'm handling this case now. So whatcha got for me?"

It felt so safe, I wanted to blurt the whole thing out. I had to force myself to say, "My dad wants me to wait until this afternoon when he can come with me to talk to you."

"Little protective, huh?"

"Just a little."

"How old are you, Laura?"

"Seventeen."

"Okay—well, you and Daddy can come in, but a detective would still talk to you alone anyway. Sometimes the presence of fathers makes kids censor themselves, you know what I mean?"

"I would say the same thing whether he was there or not," I said.

"Well, I tell you what let's do. You give me what you have and I'll follow up on it and then maybe they'll have something to tell you when you get here this afternoon."

"My father isn't going to like that."

"Why not?"

"Because he thinks my emotions are going to muddy things up and I won't just tell you the facts."

"Isn't that just like a man?" She chuckled again. "I can't force you to tell me, honey, and I sure don't want to get you in trouble with your dad. It's up to you. What time do you want to come in this afternoon?"

"Four fifteen."

"I'm off then. You'd have to talk to another one of our detectives—" "Then I'll tell you now," I said. I could hear the clicking of computer keys as I poured out the whole story, starting with the day I hit Vance's truck, then the shoplifting issue, the thing with the part in the musical, and right up to the night of the car theft. The only thing I left out was the incident in the parking lot with the Jeep, because that part was still unclear to me. When I was finished, I listened to the last clicks of the keys and the slowing down of my heart. "Good, Laura," Detective Lee said. "Now—the hard part."

I gave a weak laugh. "That wasn't the hard part?"

"I need some names, honey."

"Oh," I said.

"And I want you to know that when we question these people, your name will not be used. And we will not arrest them just on the basis of your statement—so it's not like you're throwing them in jail."

"Okay," I said

"But this does give us a lead we can follow up on. So—what's the name of the boy whose truck you ran into?"

"Vance Woodruff." There was a momentary silence. "O-kay," she said. "And the young lady who you think may have taken your keys?"

"Wendy Lewis." Another heavy pause. "And is she the same one who assisted in the shoplifting, as far as you can tell?"

"Yes, ma'am."

"And who is the girl who walked out with the stolen shirt?"

"Natalie McNair. And the other girl in the dressing room was Gigi—Virginia Palmer."

"All right. Was anybody else there the night your car was stolen?"

"Ethan Somebody. I don't know his last name."

"That's okay.

Now, Laura, is there anyone else who may have seen any of this go down, anybody who could corroborate your story?" I closed my eyes. "It's okay," she said. "Take your time. You're doing very well, by the way. I think your daddy's wrong about your emotions muddying the waters."

"Maybe somebody could tell him that this afternoon," I said.

"You know what? I think I'll stick around until ya'll come in. I'll try to work it into the conversation." She gave the chuckle I was really starting to like. "So, any other possible witnesses?"

"There could be one," I said. "But I'm not sure he really saw anything. Could I talk to him first?"

"By all means. Maybe you'll have more information for me by this afternoon, then."

"I'll try," I said.

"And when you and your father come in, I'll need you to sign this statement."

"Okay," I said. My voice was now sounding brittle, even to me.

"It's all right, Laura," she said. "You're doing the right thing. I'll make sure your daddy knows I gave you a little push here. It's hard to say no to the police, right?"

"Thank you," I said.

I barely had the receiver back in the cradle when Mom was standing at my elbow.

"I thought your father told you to wait until he went in with you," she said.

"I couldn't," I said. "You were right about the police, Mom—you don't mess around with them. She—the detective—she wanted to know right then."

Mom nodded, as if she'd had a long history of contacts with the law. "I see," she said. "You know, it isn't that Dad doesn't trust you. He just doesn't want to see you get hurt or walk into trouble without knowing it. I know it always seems like he's mad, but he's just worried."

"I'd rather see him act worried," I said. "No—I'd rather see him respect me, you know what I mean?"

"Trust me," she said, "I know what you mean." She put her

arms around me and held on tight. "I'll make sure he knows. He'll understand about the police."

"Thanks," was all I could say. I was numbed by surprise, but I may never have loved her as much as I did at that moment.

When Mom dropped me off at school that morning, both Celeste and Trent were waiting for me at my locker. It was jarring to see Trent anyplace but in the library or tucked away in the corner of some lab.

"Hi, Trent," I said, tossing question marks at Celeste with my eyes. "What's up?"

"I told him he might want to join us," Celeste said. She wiggled her eyebrows. "Just in case you had something to tell us."

Trent was blotchy from his forehead to the top of his T-shirt. Celeste was dancing around like she had to go to the bathroom.

"Would you guys both relax?" I said.

I squatted in front of my locker, and the two of them squatted with me, simultaneously, practically breathing into my ears.

"Well?" Celeste said.

"I called the police this morning, and I told them everything I know. I have to go in and sign a statement this afternoon."

"You go, girl!" Celeste said. She grabbed my head and kissed my cheek with a resounding smack.

Trent was less enthusiastic.

"What is it that you know, Laura?" he said.

"That Vance and his little cronies probably took her car," Celeste burst out in a hoarse whisper. I don't think she could help it. She'd probably been holding it back since she'd left my house the night before.

I could feel Trent gaping at me in disbelief.

"You told them that? Seriously?"

"I just gave them the facts I had," I said. "They can do what they want with them."

"You're crazy."

"She's not crazy! She's brave!" Celeste had ceased to whisper.

I stood up, and they both stood with me. I was beginning to feel like we were attached at the hips.

"I just did what I thought was right," I said.

"Is 'right' going to keep you from getting killed?"

I looked up at Trent. His eyes were blinking furiously as if his contacts were loaded with sand.

"I've known those kids all my life, Laura," he said. "I'm here to tell ya, once they find out you ratted on them, they'll never leave you alone."

I shook my head. "That's a chance I have to take."

Celeste slung her arm around my shoulder. "Told you she was brave."

"Well it's not a chance I'm taking."

"You're bailing?" Celeste said.

"No, I'm not bailing. I'm just going to be watching her back, that's all."

She pointed a finger at him. "Now that's not a bad idea. Matter of fact, I bet we could get somebody to keep an eye on her just about 24/7. I've got a lot of guy friends who—"

"Hello!"

They both turned to look at me as if they'd forgotten I was even standing there.

"What?" Celeste said.

"I SO don't need twenty-four hour protection! In the first place, I have a life-sized mental picture of Trent sitting in my living room all night with a weapon—and nothing's going to happen to me. I'm already protected."

Celeste turned to Trent. "She's talking about God."

"I don't have anything against believing in God, but all kinds of crap goes on that I don't see God putting a stop to—"

"I know what I'm doing—"

"And I know what I'm doing. Contrary to popular belief, I'm not a total nerd."

Celeste and I both stared at Trent. His voice had risen above a mumble, and the eyes, though still batting at ninety miles an hour, had a fire in them I hadn't seen before—not even when he was talking about differential calculus.

"So—what are you doing?" Celeste said.

"I'm keeping an eye on things," he said. And then he turned around, nearly knocked out two girls with his backpack, and stalked away like a bull through the brush.

"Well all right then," Celeste said. She grinned at me. "I think he's got your back, Duffy."

"It's a good thing I don't need his protection," I said. "He doesn't do well with physical confrontations, if you'll recall."

"That's what true love will do for a person."

I narrowed my eyes at her. "Don't even go there. Trent does NOT have a thing for me."

"He loves you—but not that way. Now, Joy Beth, that's another story. I seriously think he has a thing for her."

"Speaking of Joy Beth—"

Celeste was shaking her head. "She's not here again today."

I closed my locker door with my heel and started through the crowd, talking to Celeste over my shoulder. "We have to find out what's going on with her."

"I'll make a deal with you: You concentrate on what you've got coming up this afternoon, and I'll handle Joy Beth. We'll just keep each other in the loop."

I stopped—and ignored the curse of the kid who slammed into Celeste from behind and pushed her into me. "You're kind of enjoying this, aren't you?"

Celeste cocked her head. "I'm loving being able to do something that matters. I can keep twelve guys on the string at a time—but what real difference does that make? But this is huge, Duffy. It's gigantic—I'm into it up to my sombrero."

"What sombrero?"

"The one in my locker. It goes with the outfit, but my teachers won't let me wear it in class." She put her hand in the middle of my back and pushed me on. "Have you decided what to do about Owen?"

"I'm going to try to call him at work. I don't know his home number."

"You've got to get that. He sounds like great boyfriend material."

I gave her a look.

"Maybe later," she said.

Only one thing was still bothering me—talking to Owen about what he may have seen. The fact that he hadn't told me directly—that he'd slipped me a drawing instead—made me think he wasn't too excited about getting involved.

That's so strange, I thought more than once that day. *Why would he be so anxious for me to tell the police what I know and not want to do that himself?*

Still, it was as if that silken rope were still pulling me on to where I knew the details would be waiting for me. It even made it easier for me to think about how I was going to explain to Dad why I'd already told the police everything.

I just kept praying.

That afternoon our stage manager did announcements while Mr. Howitch stood in the back of the house with Natalie. She was sobbing so loudly, it was hard to focus on what Gregor was saying.

"She needs to get over it," Deirdre whispered to me. "I'm so glad she's leaving town tonight so we don't have to listen to her anymore."

"Yeah, what's that about anyway?" the girl who was playing Sandy whispered from the other side of me.

It's a last ditch effort, I wanted to say. But I kept my mouth shut and just watched the action.

Natalie had her hands clenched together at her chest, and she was actually bouncing at the knees the way Bonnie used to do when she was three and didn't get her way. By age six, of course, she knew better.

"Just a reminder, people," Gregor was saying. "Tech veek vill start on Sunday night. Rehearsals vill be at six o'clock and they vill last until ve are finish. Bring your homework to do in zee Green Room."

One of the Pink Ladies raised her hand. "And teachers don't cut us any slack just because we're a week from opening."

The other cast members all nodded to each other as if the entire faculty had their priorities completely fouled up. I was busy beating myself up for not taking care of my work situation before now.

Like I haven't had about fifty other things to think about, I told myself. *Just talk to Yolanda. She already said I was one of her best and I haven't missed a shift yet. I could even work from three o'clock until 5:45 on those days.*

It was enough of a plan to let me push that problem aside. Evidently Mr. Howitch also had taken care of HIS problem as well, because he was coming back down the aisle toward us; and Gigi and Wendy swept Natalie out the door. Just as I started to look away, Gigi caught my eye. Our gazes stuck together like a finger on an icicle.

For just an instant, a pang of frozen fear went through me. They couldn't possibly know that I'd turned them in already—could they? When they *did* find out, I would receive more than just an icy look from Gigi.

But that was what Trent had said—and I'd told him I was protected.

I have to count on God, I told myself. My mind felt for the silken rope.It was still there.

We were doing a complete run-through of the show that day, and I did the whole first act without my script. When I came off stage after my last scene, K.J. gave me a thumbs-up from the wings.

"How can you concentrate like that?" she whispered to me. "If

I'd had my car stolen, all I'd be thinking about was getting it back."

"The police are handling it," I said.

"Right. And cockroaches crawl out of my nostrils. My dad is a cop, remember?"

"I didn't know that!"

I could see K.J.'s eyebrows go up in the dimness of the wings. "He's the freakin' Chief of Police. Look— I might have a tip for you if you don't want to depend on Panama Beach's Finest."

"What kind of tip?"

"About your car." Her voice was patient, as if she were explaining trigonometry to a five year old. "A friend of mine—and I'm not going to tell you who it is, so don't ask—said she saw somebody driving a car like yours early this morning."

My mouth came open so far, I could taste the backstage dust.

"It's an '93 Volvo, right? Steel blue. Station wagon type."

"Yeah. But how did she know it was mine?"

"She didn't know for sure—not until I verified the details. Then she was positive."

I didn't ask K.J. how she knew so much about my car.

"It wasn't anybody we know," K.J. was whispering.

"Could ve have quiet backstage, please?!" Gregor called from out in the house.

K.J. nodded toward the backstage door, and I followed her outside. We both blinked against the glare of the sun on the sidewalk.

"That dude has better hearing than my dog," K.J. said. "Anyway—the guy driving it wasn't anybody we know—but maybe you do. You want the details?"

If it wasn't Vance or Ethan or one of Their Minions—then who? Maybe I was wrong—or maybe they were more devious than any of us knew.

"So?" K.J. said.

I gave her a nod out of sheer numbness.

"This guy doesn't go to 'Nama. He looked older than high school.

"It was still pretty dark, but I could tell he was wearing his hair in a ponytail."

chapter sixteen

K.J. and I froze at the same time, but I knew it was for different reasons. I was staring into the crystallized image of Ponytail Boy driving my stolen car. K.J. was obviously paralyzed by the fact that she had just given herself away.

She recovered first, rolling her oblong brown eyes as if I were the one who had exposed her. "Well, I mean, I didn't see him," she said. "My friend just told me—Look—it was just a tip, okay?"

I felt the tug, which was a surprise. This wasn't exactly a silken moment, what with K.J. boring her meaning into my forehead and tightening her teeth.

"YOU saw the guy with the ponytail, didn't you?" I said. "I didn't say that." "Yeah, you did."

"Tell the police it was me, and I'll deny it."

"Why?"

There was another eye roll, accompanied by a hair toss.

"Think about it, Duffy. It's three o'clock in the morning. On a school night. I'm down on the corner of Harrison Avenue and Fifteenth Street. Wouldn't my father, the chief of police, just love to get a hold of *that* piece of information?" She tossed her head. "Just so you know, I don't really care what my father thinks, but if he knew I sneaked out, it would mean I'd be off the stage crew so fast—and this is the only thing in this school that I can even stand, except our group thing with Mrs. I."

The brown eyes narrowed, but even as she closed them down, I could see a flicker of desperation in them. "Don't screw this up for me, okay? I was just trying to give you a lead."

She crossed her arms and I knew she was done.

"Thanks for the info," I said.

"Yeah, you look really grateful."

I shook my head. "I am—really—only it kind of messes up my theory. I think I might be in trouble."

"What kind of trouble?"

"Nothing—"

"Listen—I'm an expert on trouble. I oughta be—I've been in it enough."

She pushed her hair back with both hands and then shoved the sleeves of her black stage-crew shirt up her arms. It wouldn't have surprised me if she'd actually rolled them up, she was suddenly that into my situation.

"So what did you do?" she said.

The rope tugged at me. I glanced over both shoulders and stepped toward her. It wasn't *my* idea to share what I'd done with her—that was for sure. K.J. would have been the last person I would have taken into my confidence if it had been up to me.

"I told the police I thought it was Vance Woodruff and them that took my car—I had good reasons to think that."

"Dude—you are in trouble. Maybe—I mean don't freak out. It's just that the guy I saw driving your car—which had no license plate on it, by the way—does NOT hang out with that group."

"But do you know Them that well? Do you know everybody They know?"

"Trust me."

I could feel my eyes bulging. "You got that good a look at him at three in the morning?"

"I was right next to him at the stop light. I'm on the passenger side of the car I'm in—he's in the driver's seat of yours. I tried to memorize his face because I knew it was your car. He's definitely not their type."

I was starting to shake, and I crammed my hands into my pockets so K.J. wouldn't think I was having a breakdown. "He's not their type because he had a ponytail?"

"No. Because he didn't have an attitude. He was all serene-looking, and then he looked at me, and it was weird."

"Weird how?"

"Weird-friendly—only I didn't feel like he was trying to hit on me. He smiled, but it was, you know, hi-how-ya-doin, except not casual. See, that's the reason I looked at him so hard—because he looked at me like he knew me."

I closed my eyes so she wouldn't see how scrambled my thoughts were.

It was him. It was Ponytail Boy. Nobody else looks like that. But then what about Wendy and the keys? What about how freaked-out They were all acting that night? What about me telling on them to the police—and now they're INNOCENT?

"Hey—are you okay?" K.J. said.

"No," I said. "If Vance and those guys find out I gave information about them to the police, and they didn't do it—" I grabbed K.J. by the sleeve. "Are you SURE that was my car?"

She looked at me. I just looked back at her because I didn't know what else to do.

"Okay," she said, "I'm not saying that Vance and Ethan and whoever *didn't* steal your car. It's like SO something they would do. But this guy got it away from them or something. Maybe they sold it to him." K.J. shook her head. "But I gotta tell ya, and you can call me weird, I just know this ponytail dude does NOT know he's driving a stolen vehicle."

"You don't think so?" I said. "Really?"

The hope in my voice must have given me away because K.J.'s eyes narrowed again. "You know him?"

"I've seen him. I don't actually know him."

"Only it feels like you do."

Our gazes locked. Both of us were nodding at the same time.

"So—can you figure out how he got mixed up in this?" she said.

"No. Right now, I can't figure anything out."

"Sorry I messed up your head." To my surprise, her eyes softened.

"I have to go sign my statement at the police station after rehearsal," I said, "and now I don't know what to do."

"You want some advice?"

I nodded. I could listen to it—that didn't mean I had to take it.

"When you go to the cops, don't even tell them about the guy I saw. In the first place, they're gonna think you're weird. And besides, I can't testify so what would be the point? You can see that, right?"

"I can see that you don't want to get kicked off stage crew, and I don't want you to."

We did our twin-nod again.

"And you know what, I don't really like the idea of getting Vance and them off the hook, either," she said. "Those people are demon seed or something."

I sighed. "I guess all I can do is tell the police what I know. That's what I did this morning."

"And you won't bring my name into it?"

"What good would it do?"

K.J. gave me a smile and then pulled it back in.

"Can I ask you something?" I said.

"Go ahead."

"If you want to stay on stage crew so much, why do you do things that are sure to get you thrown off if you get caught—like sneak out at night?"

I watched her neck stiffen. "It's a chance I gotta take," she said.

"But why?"

"Let's just say if I don't, I'll go insane."

Then K.J. disappeared through the door.

By the time we got to notes at the end of practice, I felt like I was falling off a cliff, without a rope of ANY kind.

It didn't help that Dad was more than a little tense when he picked me up after rehearsal. It was obvious Mom had told him I'd already told the detective everything, and MORE than obvious that she hadn't been successful in making him see things from my point of view. He drove like the Terminator all the way to the police station.

God, hello—are you there? I thought. *Are you taking a coffee break or something? Where's my rope?*

"I talked to that Detective Lee," he said finally. "She recorded your voice and compared it to a tape of an anonymous call they got last night from some girl giving them information about your car theft. Said she knew who did it and gave them the same names you gave them this morning. Naturally they were a little suspicious." Dad shot me a look that told me "they" weren't the only ones.

"It wasn't me," I said.

"They know that now."

"Why did they even think that? Why would I do that?"

"Because evidently there is reason to be intimidated by these kids—the names you gave them. Are you, Laura?"

"Am I what?" I said, although I knew. I just needed a second or two to regroup.

He gave me the sigh I expected. "Are you afraid of these kids you think took your car?"

"I used to be." *And now I am again! Why did K.J. have to tell me that stuff about Ponytail Boy?*

"Why? Do they carry guns?"

"No!"

"Then what possible reason could you have—?"

"Because they do bad stuff, Dad." I knew my voice lacked the required respect, but I was beyond worrying about it.

"What kind of 'stuff'? What do they do?"

There was no sign of the rope, but I knew what I had to do. I was too far into this to start lying or holding back now. I gave him a quick rendition of what Celeste had told me. He glanced at me several times during my spiel—as if he were actually listening to me.

"I know it's all hearsay," I said when I got to the end. "But there isn't any reason not to believe it."

"Sounds like a bunch of spoiled brats to me." Dad pulled into a parking place and threw the car into PARK. "What I don't understand is why you didn't tell us about all this stuff before."

I did consider holding back then. I thought about shrugging it off because what good would it do to tell him?

And then I felt the tug, a soft one.

"Because you really don't listen to me," I said. "I start to tell you things and you cut me off like you already know what I'm going to say—and you almost never do."

He didn't say anything. He just took off his sunglasses, dropped them into his shirt pocket, and opened the car door.

"All right. Let's go in and get this over with."

But HOW am I going to get it over with? I thought as I followed him through the police station lobby. I still had no idea what I was going to do about Ponytail Boy, in spite of my promise to K.J. not to rat on her. But K.J. wasn't holding the other end of my rope.

Just don't let go, God, I prayed. *Just please don't let go.*

Detective Lee was a tall lady with a face like the front of a Mack truck. She told Dad to get himself a cup of coffee and whisked me away to a cinderblock room with a large "mirror" on one wall.

Scenes from every police show I'd ever seen sprang into my head, with the D.A. watching through a one-way mirror while investigators leaned over the suspect, screaming at her until she begged for her lawyer.

"Don't let the interrogation room freak you out," the detective said as she nodded me in. "Honest, Laura, you are not under suspicion."

I sank into the plastic seat and felt absolutely like I was. She sat across from me and smiled. Her eyes twinkled as they all but disappeared into her cheeks.

"Did your father fill you in on the two tape recordings?" I grunted a yes. She smiled deeper.

"Reason number one why he isn't sitting here with you—I didn't think you'd mind."

She kept smiling as she booted up a computer and handed me a tiny microphone that was attached to it. "We have to double check everything—more to determine whether we might have a witness rather than to 'nail' you. Besides, there's actually nothing illegal about giving an anonymous tip."

"Really?" I said. I knew I sounded a little too interested in that piece of information, but if she picked up on it, she didn't let on.

"We just need your help to figure out who our other informant is."

"Why?" I said.

"Because it sounds like she knows more than she's telling."

I nodded, though I wasn't sure why. I had no idea what to think much less what to say. One thing was giving me hope, though. If there was nothing wrong with an anonymous tip, K.J. could call in, disguise her voice, and as long as they didn't pass it on to the chief of police.

But I still couldn't imagine K.J. doing that. As it was, I felt like any minute this detective person was going to see that I wasn't giving her ALL the information I had, and it made me want to throw up.

I was no longer being pulled by the silken rope. I was tied up in it.

God—please—show me what to do!

But I knew I didn't need God to show me—because He already had. I could almost hear Him saying, *Don't make me repeat myself,*

Laura: You tell what you know and you let the police take care of it—and I will take care of you.

"Now I'm going to have you listen to the tape of the anonymous caller and see if you recognize her voice," Detective Lee was saying." She put her hand in the pocket of her blazer.

"Okay," I said. "But—um—there's something else I found out this afternoon. Do you want to hear it?"

She took her hand out of the pocket and said, "Shoot."

"This girl," I said, "She told me that at about three o'clock this morning she saw some guy driving my car, right down on Fifteenth and Harrison—only it wasn't Vance or Ethan or any of them. In fact, she's sure he doesn't even go to our school. She said he looked too old anyway."

The smile left the detective's face as abruptly as it had appeared there. If I wasn't suddenly under suspicion, you could have fooled me.

"What are you doing, Laura?" she said.

"Ma'am?"

"Are you trying to back down on this?"

"No! I'm just telling you what I was told. I thought you'd want to know everything."

"Who is this girl who gave you this information?"

"I can't tell you her name."

"Why?"

"Because she'll get in trouble. She was out at three in the morning!"

"Are you the girl?"

"No, ma'am!"

Detective Lee moved to a spot on the table directly over me and planted herself there. I was forced to look up into black eyes that were suddenly penetrating.

"Did somebody get to you?" she said.

"Get to me? I don't understand."

She folded her arms across her wide chest—looking up at her was now like staring at an impenetrable wall.

"We've heard the names Vance Woodruff and Ethan Powell and Virginia Palmer and the rest of them around here before. They've been accused of everything from petty theft to aggravated assault. But the minute we get close to picking them up, oddly enough the charges are suddenly dropped and the case evaporates into thin air." She leaned in closer. "I think Mr. Woodruff and his friends have an intimidation factor that nobody can get past."

"That isn't it!" I said. "It was at first, but not now. Honest."

She looked at me as if my own guilt were plastered all over my face. But I knew the only thing on me was disbelief. How could she think I was lying when I was working so hard to tell the truth?

"Don't jerk us around, Laura," she said. "You don't do that with the law."

"I know—and I'm not!"

"Are you now saying Vance Woodruff didn't take your car?"

"No, ma'am. I'm just saying somebody saw a person who isn't part of Vance's group driving it. That doesn't change what I've already told you."

"You would still testify to what you've said in your statement in a court of law?"

"Testify?" I said, my heart beating out of my chest.

"If it should come to that."

"I guess so," I said.

"But your 'friend' wouldn't testify to what she saw?"

"She can't."

"She won't."

Detective Lee put her hand in the pocket of her blazer once more and pulled out a small tape recorder.

"All right," she said as she inserted the tape into it. Her voice was bristly. "I want you to listen to this and tell me if you recognize this voice."

I nearly choked when I heard the voice saying, "I know who took Laura Duffy's Volvo. You should question Vance Woodruff, Ethan Powell, Virginia Palmer, Natalie McNair, and Wendy Lewis."

"May I have your name please?" said an adult voice.

"No," said Stevie. "I can't."

Detective Lee punched the STOP button, her eyes still on me as if she might miss a clue on my face if she glanced away for a fraction of a second.

"There seems to be an epidemic of cowardice among the teenagers in this town," Detective Lee said. "I hope you haven't caught it, Laura. Do you know that voice?"

"I think so," I said. "I can't be absolutely sure."

"Who do you think it is?"

I knew I couldn't hesitate or she'd bore right into my brain with her eyes.

"I'm pretty sure it's Stevie—Stephanie—Martinez."

"She's a friend of yours?"

"She's just in one of my classes. She used to be friends with Ethan and them—only she doesn't hang around them anymore. She wasn't shoplifting and she wasn't there at the mall the night my car was stolen."

Detective Lee was nodding slowly, her gaze still on me, "All right," she said. "I know it's hard getting your peers involved—but the so-called 'code of silence' among you kids makes it impossible to nail the bad guys."

"Can I say something else?" I said.

"Talk to me."

"I don't even care if I ever see that car again. I just don't want to be like them."

"You're taking a good step away from that. Who knows, you could see justice done and maybe get your car back, too."

"Do you want the details about the guy my friend saw this morning—?"

"No," she said. "Without a statement from her, we have nothing to go on. Speaking of which, I need you to sign yours."

She pushed a typed form toward me and handed me a pen. "Jot down everything you just told me, date it, and sign it."

I knew she was dismissing Ponytail Boy completely from her mind.

I did all I could do, I told myself as I followed her out to the waiting area. *Aren't I supposed to feel better now?*

I might have if my father hadn't been pacing around with an empty Styrofoam cup with a bite taken out of its rim. At least Detective Lee went straight to him and explained everything, leaving out K.J.'s "tip" as if I'd never brought it up.

"Be proud of her," she said to Dad as she stuck her hand out for him to shake. "She's doing the right thing."

"Are you all right?" Dad asked as we drove home.

"I'm fine."

"Let me ask you a question," Dad said. "You seem pretty confident about pointing the finger at these kids."

"I'm not exactly pointing the finger—"

"Call it whatever you want, Laura. The upshot is they'll be brought in for questioning based on what you've told the police. My questions is—are you doing this to get back at them for giving you a bad time?"

I gritted my teeth and stared straight ahead.

"I'm just asking," Dad said. "It's only human to want revenge."

I pried my molars apart. "I don't hate them. I just don't want to be like them." Dad gave a short laugh. "You don't want to be rich, popular—" "Not if it means also being snotty and cruel and thinking my rights are being violated if I don't get my own way." He nodded at the windshield. There was a tensing of the tired lines around his mouth and his eyes.

"I want to tell you something," I said. "I hate working at the Gap. I'll find some other way to pay you back for having my car fixed— I know I still owe you, but working there throws me right in the middle of every thing I despise."

"What exactly do you despise?"

"People spending all this money buying more and more new stuff so they'll look like everybody else. My real friends don't even shop there because they're authentic. And I hate people lying to get out of working and people stealing. It's just—I don't know how to put it—"

"It's toxic."

I stared at him.

"Yeah," I said. "That's exactly it."

Dad gave me a sideways glance. "I heard that on a radio talk-show. I never thought I'd hear it coming out of my mouth."

"So—you get it."

"I think so. Anyway, I don't want you in that mall parking lot at night anymore. It's too dangerous."

"Then it's okay if I go ahead and let the store know I'm quitting?" I said.

"Call them the minute you get home," he said. I didn't give him a chance to change his mind. After he parked the van in the driveway, I went straight for the phone and dialed the number.

Yolanda's voice was so icy it was like opening a door in the frozen foods department. "This is Laura Duffy," I said. There was a short silence.

"Laura," she said finally. Her voice thawed a little. "I was just going to call you."

"Oh," I said. "Well—I'm supposed to come in tonight."

"I know. I was going to tell you not to."

"Oh," I said again. "Well—I was calling you to tell you that I need to quit. I'm sorry. I know you said I was one of your best and I appreciate that, but I just can't—"

"Save your breath." Yolanda's voice had frozen again, and each word was like an ice cube chinking into a frosted glass. "I'm cleaning house anyway. I was going to call you to tell you that I'm letting all of my high school staff go."

"Go?" I said. "You mean, like, fired?"

"Exactly. I've been losing inventory over the last month—as in theft—and it could only be happening with help from the inside. There is no way I could get to the bottom of it unless one of you was willing to expose one of your little friends, and I don't see that happening, so there you are."

I was staring, unseeing, at my mother's kitchen bulletin board. I closed my eyes.

"I'm not one of Them," I said. "As a matter of fact—"

"I never thought you were—until just now, when you suddenly decided to quit out of the clear blue."

"It's not out of the blue! I've already told the—"

"Listen, I'd love to chat," Yolanda said. The ice cubes belied every word. "But I have a nasty list of phone calls ahead of me."

"I can tell you who—"

But she'd hung up. The French manicured nails were probably already tapping out someone else's number. Maybe Wendy's. Or Owen's.

chapter seventeen

It helped that practically the minute I called Celeste, she was there, overnight bag in hand, and that I had the whole K.J. thing to fill her in on, and the scene at the police station.

"You think the guy K.J. saw—what do you call him?"

"Ponytail Boy."

"You think the same guy who keeps coming to your rescue has ripped off your car?"

"No. But I believe K.J. . Why would she make that up?"

"That still doesn't mean Vance and his little minions didn't do it. You can't tell me they aren't guilty as sin—especially with Stevie herself telling on them."

"I'm leaving that to the police."

"You're forgetting one thing, though."

"What?"

"Hello—Owen. What about the drawing?"

I sat up. "Yikes! I was gonna call him at work and then with all this other stuff happening—"

"Is he working tonight?"

"I don't know."

Celeste scrambled off the bed and got her cell phone out of her bag.

"I'll call—just in case that witchy-woman answers." She wiggled her eyebrows at me. "I've still got the number on speed dial. Am I good or what?"

"Erase it after this call," I said. "It's probably a curse."

Celeste held up a finger to me, but her brow immediately smoothed out.

"Is this Owen?" she said. Pause. "This is Ms. Duffy's personal secretary. Would you hold for her, please?"

She handed the phone to me, grinning. I was grinning myself.

"You're still there!" I said.

"Unfortunately. It's about as friendly as the surface of the moon here without you."

I grinned even bigger.

He lowered his voice. "Look, I can't talk right now. We're so understaffed it isn't funny. You want to meet me during dinner break tomorrow night?"

"Okay."

"I'll buy, if you don't eat too much—like you would. Rabbits eat more than you do."

The smile that played at my lips as I hung up felt soft.

"Ooh, Duffy."

Celeste's eyebrows were going at full tilt.

"What?" I said. "*What?*"

"I know that look."

I got up on my knees so I could see myself in the mirror over my dresser.

"What look?"

"You like that boy. Don't take me there."

We crawled under the covers, and I snapped off the light.

"What about your homework?" Celeste muttered sleepily.

"What about yours?"

She didn't answer, and I lay there listening to her deep, even breathing.

For the first time in my life, grades didn't seem that important. Neither did my stolen car. And neither did getting fired before I could quit, even if it was Wendy's fault. What was important was so very real. And I knew I would be led to it by that same force that had gotten me this far.

Which was why I went to Mrs. Isaacsen before school the next morning.

"And then she wasn't here for me to talk to her at all. She stopped coming to school."

"I feel like that's my fault."

"Talk to me."

"I'm feeling Him," I said.

"Feeling God," she said.

I nodded,

"I feel Him pulling me along—and I'm going—only He's not pulling me out—He's pulling me in deeper."

"Tell me," she said.

"The bell's gonna ring."

"That's why God gave guidance counselors late passes. Do you have a test first period?"

"No."

"Then keep talking."

So I did. I told her everything—and when I was through, I said, "You see what I mean? I'm getting deeper into everything and I can't get out."

"Maybe you don't need to get out."

"But I want to! I want all of this to be over."

"Then you don't want the next key to more power?"

"Yes!"

She smiled at me. "But a key lets you in, not out."

I looked at the tiny silver key on my bracelet as the last of the tears trailed down into my mouth. I licked the salt on my lips and watched Mrs. I. open a desk drawer and pull out her copy of *The Message*. It seemed to open to exactly the page she wanted, and she closed her eyes over it for a second. I could feel the rope resting in the hands of my mind.

She perched her glasses on her nose. "First Corinthians 2:7," she said. "'God's wisdom is something mysterious that goes deep into the interior of His purposes.'"

She looked at me over the half-specs, her eyes at last twinkling in her way of wisdom. "I don't see anything here about God getting you *out* of something. I think He wants you smack in the middle of it."

"So it's still about surrendering."

"It's about allowing yourself to be disciplined to follow where God is leading you. You're doing that."

"You kind of told me that before, only I didn't get it. Getting discipline is a power?"

"*Being* disciplined is a power. The key to it is obedience, and it seems to me that's what you're about."

"But I don't see what good it's doing! I've lost my car—I've lost my job—"

"Were those treasures you really wanted?"

"No." I could feel my forehead folding into furrows the size of licorice ropes. "But what about me trying to tell that detective the truth and ending up having her all over me because she thinks I'm trying to back out. And then none of that seems like it even matters if Joy Beth doesn't come out of her depression. I'd rather have her back than my stupid car!"

"Everything you're doing is right, though, and that's God working in you. Your spirit is being led by His spirit—your two spirits are in open communion. It isn't up to you to figure out where this is all going. The whole point is to go where God leads and leave the journey up to Him—including the destination."

I let that sink in. "Do you think He wants me to tell Detective Lee that it was K.J. who told me about Ponytail Boy?"

Mrs. I. made a pained face. "That's a tough one. I'd say keep praying about it—maybe talk to K.J. again. If you're not sure where God's leading, then just wait until you are."

"Until that silky rope pulls me," I said.

She nodded as if she knew exactly what I was talking about.

The rope somehow pulled me through the day and through our last rehearsal before Sunday night would start tech week. By the end of notes, I was also feeling something else. There were butterflies in my stomach because I was meeting Owen later that night.

This is stupid, I kept telling myself. *Owen and I are just good friends. What's this about all of a sudden?*

He already had a table saved for us at the far end of the food court, and there was a heaping serving of slippery-looking nachos waiting for me. He stood up when he saw me, his hand jingling change in his pocket.

"Hey," he said. "Let me get you something to drink."

"I'm fine," I said. I slid into the seat.

"You sure?"

"Positive."

He sat down. He nudged the nachos in my direction and folded and unfolded his hands on the table, then put them in his lap where he proceeded to rub his palms up and down on his thighs.

Is he nervous? I thought. *Yikes—he's making ME nervous!*

And then it came to me: *He figures I've found the drawing by now, and he knows why I'm here.*

I felt suddenly sad. I would much rather be talking to Owen about college or Queen Yo-Yo or even his recent break-up with Genevieve. I wanted to hear him laugh and watch him draw pictures. And have him put his arm around my shoulders.

I could feel my cheeks warming up. I hooked my hair behind my ears.

"You okay?" he said.

"Sure," I said.

He poked at a tortilla chip but he didn't pick it up.

"Are you okay?" I said.

"No. I'm hating life right now."

"Because of Genevieve?"

Owen blinked, as if I'd just spoken to him in Czechoslovakian. His hair was a soft brown color tonight, normal looking. The lack of gel made him look vulnerable. That, and the way he was priming his drink through the plastic top with his straw.

"No, it's not Genevieve," he said finally. " I'm okay with that."

"That's good," I said.

I wished I had let him get me a drink so I'd have something to do with my hands. I could have dug into the nachos, but the way the grease was pooling on top of the cheese was making my stomach squirm.

"Okay, Laura" Owen said. "There's an elephant sitting here in the middle of the table and we're both pretending it isn't there."

The laugh that burst out of me was more from relief than hilarity.

"So go for it," he said.

"Okay—well—"

"No, let me go first. You have to. I'm older."

I nodded"Look," he said, "you shouldn't have been fired. If you'd told Yolanda when you overheard Wendy and them in the dressing room, you wouldn't have been. I'm afraid I influenced you against doing that, and I feel like a jerk."

"You are SO not a jerk! Besides—I don't want the stupid job anyway."

"Yeah, but I want you to have the stupid job. I'm hating it without you there."

Our glances clinked together. His blue eyes were soft and shy, and they darted away from my face to the nachos.

"You're the only thing I miss about it," I said.

"You could come back, you know. All you have to do is turn Wendy in."

"I tried to tell Yolanda the truth yesterday when I called to quit, but she listens about as well as my father does. I did tell the police about it, though. Only they were more interested in hearing what I said about Them stealing my car."

He looked up from the nachos. "That's what I was hoping you'd do."

"I wouldn't have done it if it weren't for you. Without your drawing, I never would have figured out that my keys were in my jacket pocket when I got to work, but they were in my purse when you walked me out that night. Somebody moved them." I looked straight into his eyes. "You think it was Wendy, don't you?"

He nodded slowly.

I moved the nachos aside so I could lean in.

"You saw her take them out of my pocket," I said.

He tried to grin. "Did I say that?"

"You didn't have to. Come on, Owen, you saw me getting them out of my purse, but you drew Wendy taking them out of my jacket—so you had to have seen her."

Owen pulled his eyes from mine. "You usually keep them in your jacket. You jingle when you walk. I guess I just—"

"Did you see Wendy take them out of my pocket?"

He still wouldn't look at me. "What did you tell the police?"

"I didn't give them your name."

Owen let out a long breath and sank against the chair back, one shoulder higher than the other.

"If you told them about the keys being moved, that's probably all they need anyway," he said.

"They want all the proof they can get."

"What I saw doesn't really prove anything."

"Then you did see her."

He closed his eyes.

"Owen." I clutched the sides of the table. "You're the one who told me I didn't have to have proof to go to the police with what I know."

"I know I did." Owen's chin was nearly down to his chest, and his mouth was pulled forward into a bunch.

"Are you afraid of something?" I said.

He did a reverse-sniff through his nostrils. "Yeah. I don't have your guts."

"But there's nothing to be scared of! That Detective Lee woman I talked to was pretty intense, but—"

"I can't talk to the police."

Owen sat up and hung his head over his hands, which he folded in front of him, thumbs twitching. "I knew if I gave you the drawing, you'd figure it out and you'd have enough to go to the cops. I didn't think they'd want more. It's not like this is brain surgery."

"They're not going to tell Their Royal Highnesses who snitched on them, if that's what you're worried about—"

"The only reason I ever gave those little punks a second thought was because I was concerned about what they could do to you. I don't give a flip about them."

I was sure my forehead looked like it was tied into a square knot.

"Then I don't get it. You know what a wimp I am, and if I can go talk to the cops—"

"First of all, you're not a wimp." Both Owen's voice and his eyes were suddenly sharp as he looked at me with something bordering on anger. "You're the coolest chick I know. I knew that with a little push you'd turn that whole lousy crowd in. But that's all I can do for you, Laura. I'm sorry."

"I don't understand."

"Then let me spell it out for you." Owen now leaned toward me so that our noses were almost touching. His words came out in low, hot blasts. "If I have to go to court and testify to something I saw while I was working at the Gap, my old man is going to find out I've got a job, and that isn't the agreement we 'worked out.'" His eyes narrowed to resentful points. "He'll pull my college funding so I won't be able to finish school, I'll end up in a dead-end job like I've got right now, and then I won't be able to give my mother the money she needs to just exist—money my dad won't give her—and I'll wind up being a jerk like him." He glanced at his wrist as if there were a watch there and launched himself out of the chair. "I've gotta get back. I'll see you."

As I watched him walk away, I knew my chin was hanging halfway to my belly.

No, Owen, I thought. *I'm the jerk.*

chaptereighteen

All through the weekend, it was as if the rope I was depending on was dangling somewhere out of my reach. The only thing that got me through was the echo of Mrs. Isaacsen saying, *If you're not sure where God's leading, then just wait until you are.*

So I tried to focus on getting ahead on homework and psyching myself up for the start of tech week.

It doesn't seem fair, I told God late Friday night. *I want to sing on stage more than anything else in the world, and now I can't even enjoy it. I hate it that this whole stupid car thing has taken that away from me. I might as well have given the part back to Natalie for all the fun I'm getting out of it right now. I guess They stole that from me, too.*

That sounded so much like whining. I tossed and turned most of the night, praying a thousand times for God to lower my safe, silky rope to me. Saturday morning I crawled out of bed when it was still gray and misty and hauled my Bible and my journals down to the Bay.

There was no one out yet, and it was easy to forget the few cars swishing by on Beach Street. It was as if they were trying to be quiet so I could finally find some peace. I let my back relax against the bench and tried to pretend I was sitting in God's hand.

Above me, a circle of gulls was crying.

That's the way I must sound to God about now, I thought.

I swept the horizon with my eyes and tried to shut myself up.

Out at the end of the pier, a row of pelicans stood, methodically cleaning under their wings. *At least they have something they can DO*, I thought. Okay—more whining.

You've got stuff you can do, Laura. Come on, quit your cryin'.

I gave the gull-circle a hard glare and then dug into my backpack for my copy of *The Message*. Okay—what was that passage Mrs. I. read to me? It made some sense. First Corinthians something—

I thumbed my way there and finally found it.

God's wisdom is something mysterious that goes deep into the interior of His purposes.

I looked back at the pelicans and grunted.

Maybe I should be trying to dig the rope OUT instead of trying to jump UP for it, I thought. *That's why I can't feel the tug. It's way deep in there.*

I leaned back and felt the stillness. I closed my eyes.

I wish it were this still inside me, God. Maybe if You would just take me in where it's quiet, I would see that silky piece of rope and I could grab onto it and get moving again. Stay. Stay where you are.

I flinched. Was it the breeze? There was no breeze.

Was it the Whisper?

I waited, but there was only the stillness.

So I whispered. "I'll obey whatever You tell me to do. But please—just tell me. Let me hear You. Let me feel You pulling me."

Stay. Stay.

I opened my eyes and strained to see something, like maybe the words just disappearing on a breath. There were only the pelicans, now puffed up and sleeping. And one gull had found something to eat in a tide pool and seemed to be savoring it. Without a sound.

"I'll stay, God," I whispered. "Until You show me where to go." I went home a while later and outlined the paper I had to write for Mrs. Wren on The Great Gatsby, although it was hard to focus. Almost every character in the book reminded me of Them, grabbing for everything they wanted, no matter how much it hurt somebody else. By about one o'clock that afternoon, I couldn't stand any of Them any longer. I did finish the thing Sunday afternoon, and then I stretched out on the bed and prayed one more time, *Please God—please God—please—pull me. Take me in, lead me out, I don't care what You do, just show me, please!*

The next thing I knew, Mom was shaking me. "Isn't your rehearsal at six o'clock?" she said.

I blinked at her.

"Honey, it's half-past five…"

"No!"

I scrambled out of bed, hair flying one way, legs the other.

"Take the van," she said. "I'll fix you something to eat to take with you—"

I left the house with enough ham and Swiss on rye to feed the entire cast. Visions of Mr. Howitch perched like a vulture above me and pointing to his watch were in my head as I made a mad dash to the school, wheeling the van into a parking place outside the theatre building just as the numbers on the dashboard clock flipped over to 5:45.

If I RUN to the dressing room I MIGHT make it into costume for the first act, I thought. *Forget make-up…*

I tried to scramble out of the car without unbuckling the seatbelt. I stopped and closed my eyes and tried to breathe like a normal person.

Okay, okay—don't freak. It's not the total end of the world—

I calmed down enough to press the button on the seatbelt and lower myself out of the van. I even took the time to lock it up with the key.

Okay—it's all about Rizzo and Grease *now*, I told myself. *There's nothing I can do about anything else right now. I have to take one responsibility at a time.*

It sounded so adult, I wanted to congratulate myself. I turned to hurry toward the theatre—and Wendy stepped right into my path. I gasped—audibly—the way they do in old black-and-white horror movies. "Sorry," she said. "I didn't mean to freak you out. Can we talk for a minute?" "No," I said. "I have to get to rehearsal." I didn't add that I couldn't imagine her saying anything that I would want to listen to. Especially when she was wearing that Styrofoam smile. "I'll walk up with you, then," she said. I shrugged and stalked on toward the theatre. What the HECK was this about? Whatever it was, it was already ticking me off. To say that I was completely over Them and their power trip was the understatement of the millennium.

"So—did Yolanda call you and fire you?" she said.

I nodded.

"Me, too."

I grunted.

"So you never told her you thought it was me that pulled that-shoplifting thing."

"No," I said, my teeth welded together. "I didn't tell her—"

"That's good, because I didn't do it. A bunch of us think it's really unfair that she fired everybody for something she probably did herself, so we're holding a meeting—"

I stopped and stared at her. That was when I saw how fast her eyes were blinking, and how hard she was licking her lips to get some moisture going in her mouth. She wasn't as good at pretending to care about somebody else as I'd once suspected Stevie was. The chick was a basket case.

"You're kidding me, right?" I said.

"Yeah, she is," said a voice behind me. "But I'm not."

I whirled around and found myself nose-to-nose with Gigi. Her eyes were like bullets. "I don't know who you think you are," she said, "but you're about to find out how much power you *don't* have around here."

I waited for fear to clutch me, but it didn't. Not until I felt hands grab my arms from behind and ram me back against a hard torso—and then I saw a black truck peel around the corner of the building with a square head sitting behind the wheel.

I'd seen that head coming at me before.

But this time the features didn't distort into a twisted version of what was real. I knew it was Vance—and I knew it was Natalie who jumped out of the passenger side when he screeched to a stop inches from me—and I knew it was Ethan who threw me into the back seat of the cab and climbed in behind me.

Vance leaned across the seat toward the window on the passenger side. "Me and Ethan got it from here," he said.

"Thanks, babe," Gigi said. "But Wendy's coming with you."

"No way."

"She can't come with us. Look at her—she's flipping out."

Vance swore and leaned further toward the window. "Go home, Wendy. You're out of this."

"No!"

"Do it, Wendy," I heard myself shouting at her. "You don't want any part of Them—"

There was more swearing then, and Ethan yanked me back by the shoulders—but not fast enough to get me out of the path of something hard and brutal that slammed into the side of my face.

That was the last thing I saw until my eyes opened to a blur of hardwood above me. Once the world came into focus again, that blur became a low ceiling.

"See that?" I heard Vance say. "She's coming to. I told you I didn't hit her that hard."

"Why'd you have to hit her at all? I had it handled."

I assumed that was Ethan, although I'd never pegged him for a whiner. His voice was high and thin, as if he were on the edge of tears.

"This got way out of control," he said.

"Shut up, man."

I felt something lurch, and my body rocked back and forth. Actually, the entire surface I was lying on rocked with the floor. It was some kind of bed, which Vance sat on beside me. I cringed and turned my head away. It felt like the side of my face was caving in.

"Are we on a boat?" I said. I started to sit up, but he put his hand in the middle of my chest and pushed me down.

"What are you doin'?" Ethan said.

"I'm tryin' to get it back in control." He swore again.

I'd never realized how cussing could split your eardrum down the middle. I wanted to crawl up into the corner of the cabin we were in and hide myself from it, from him, from both of them. And then I felt a pull—soft and silken and smooth—and I stopped wanting and I stopped thinking and I just followed.

"Get away from me," I said. "I can't stand to have you anywhere near me."

"You'll get used to me—"

"No stinkin' way—and don't even think about calling me anything except Laura."

Vance's face loomed right over mine, his breath reeking of cinnamon gum and beer. "How 'bout I call you Loser? Laura the Loser—that's what my girls call you."

"Your 'girls'?" I said. That was more disgusting to me than the cussing.

"Yeah. My Girls. They do whatever I want—and you will, too, if you've got any brains."

I just looked at him. I didn't have to imagine his head morphing into a giant block and his ears pulling outward, distorting his eyes into ugly slits—because he actually looked like that. I might have retched, having him that close to me, if I hadn't been pulled back into a cautious place.

"So—you gonna cooperate?" he said.

"Depends on what you want me to do," I said.

He hissed through his teeth. "What I want you to do is *nothing*. Just sit here and shut up until—"

He jerked his head toward Ethan.

"What?" Ethan said.

His voice was sullen, and I stole a glance at him. He was sitting on a low, built-in chest, chewing on a toothpick.

"We're here until when?" Vance said. "What time?"

"I don't know. Whenever."

Whenever. Whenever the rehearsal was over. The rehearsal I was missing. The rehearsal where Natalie had conveniently reappeared.

"Hey, man—" Vance said between his teeth.

There was more swearing, and Vance rocked the boat as he jerked himself off the bed. I sat up, and then steeled myself against the wave of dizziness that all but knocked me onto my back again. I wasn't about to keep lying there looking up at Vance like some quivering little lump of jelly. I wasn't one of his "girls."

"You in this or not?" The veins on Vance's neck were bulging bigger and harder than his tendons as he punched his face close to Ethan's.

"I don't know. Am I? So far you've changed everything around the way *you* want it, so whaddya need me for?"

"Like what? What have I changed?"

"Like nobody said anything about slappin' her around."

"What was I supposed to do—let her run her fat mouth?"

"I had it handled!"

"If you had, she never woulda got a word out!"

"So like you always do—you just took over. We had to do it YOUR way. Those are YOUR girls. What am I?"

It finally dawned on me that the conversation was no longer about me. In fact, they'd probably forgotten I was even there—for the moment. I took that moment to ease myself off the bed and inch along the side of the cabin toward an open passageway. My head was pounding, and I actually did think I was going to throw up, but I focused on that opening, taking tiny step after tiny sideways step. There was no motor running. The boat didn't seem to be moving except to rock in place. If we were still tied up, I could jump to a dock and run in the direction of the school—and THEN I could throw up.

Just as long as Vance and Ethan kept arguing like a pair of little playground bullies, I could keep moving. I only had about ten more sideways slides to go.

"If you'd come up with something that wasn't lame once in a while," Vance was saying into Ethan's flared nostrils, "maybe we'd do it your way."

"Lame!"

"Yeah. 'I got the perfect place to hide the car, man. And what happens?"

"Somebody coulda took it from anyplace. Besides, now we don't gotta deal with that heap anymore. Cops question us—we're not lyin' if we say we don't know where it is."

"Since when did we worry about lyin', man? And not bein' able to get our hands on the car screws up the whole plan."

I was almost to the passageway. One more slide and I could run—and not just run to rehearsal—run to Detective Lee with all the information they'd just spit out right there for me to hear. But if I had ALL the information—the "whole plan"—I would really have something to run with. I held my breath and stayed.

"You talk about a lame plan," Ethan said. "Like they were ever gonna believe she stole her own car and tried to pin it on us."

"What else were we gonna do? Wendy's the one that screwed up with the keys. We're done with her. We're gettin' rid of her."

"You gonna give her a concussion, too?"

That was it. That was all I needed. My toes were inches from the doorway.

But there was dead silence. Still moving sideways I watched their heads turn toward the bed suddenly remembering. I dove through the doorway, arms flailing against the sides of the narrow passage, flinging myself at a ladder that reached up to freedom. Hands grabbed onto the waistband of my jeans and yanked me backwards.

There was nothing I could do but scream.

chapter nineteen

I screamed, loud, raspy, angry screams, until I was thrown back down on the bed. Then I found out I could do something else. I put my foot in the middle of Vance's chest, and I shoved. It caught him off balance, long enough for me to roll off and scramble again for the doorway, still yelling through blinding white pain.

Ethan tackled me from behind and pushed me face first into the floor. He found my mouth with his hand and smashed it in. With his lips close to my ear he hissed, "Shut up."

But I didn't. I couldn't. His wrist was digging into my face where Vance had hit me before, and I couldn't have held back my screams if I'd wanted to.

Ethan managed to keep them muffled while Vance's banging around and swearing faded to someplace above us.

"What are you doing?" Ethan shouted to him.

"Gettin' outa here before she brings the cops down on us—"

There was more swearing, and then the rumble of a motor.

It was now Ethan's turn to swear. His fingers loosened enough for me to get my mouth open partway and chomp down on a couple of them. Then he out-cussed Vance as he got off of me and tore for the passageway. The boat lurched, and I could hear him swearing his way up the ladder.

When I could tell he'd gone to the front of the boat, I got to my feet and took off down the passageway again. Just as I reached the ladder, the boat swung to the side and hurled me up against the hardwood paneling. I groped for the rungs and clawed my way up. Over the roar of the engine I could hear Vance and Ethan screaming at each other, though their words were whipped away on the wind as the boat left the dock behind.

I screamed a useless, "No!" out of a mouth I could barely open for the pain and crawled for the back of the boat. The bow was rising like it was climbing steps, and I slid the last few feet and hoisted myself up onto the padded benches that lined the stern. By now the sunset was completely gone, and the water churning below me was inky black. But the voices coming from the direction of the steering wheel were blacker, and I had to get away from them.

Grabbing onto the rail, I brought one knee up over it. But even as I leaned forward, arms folded around me from behind and once again I was flattened to the deck.

"Let go of me!" I screamed. "Let—go!"

I couldn't pull myself loose enough to kick him, but I was able to jab my elbow into his stomach. Soft flesh gave way beneath it—and I knew it wasn't Vance or Ethan who was holding me. Struggling like a slippery fish in his grasp, I got my face around in time to see Trent saying "SHHHHH!" with his too-small mouth.

I stopped screaming and went limp against him. He swayed for a second, and then rolled me like a sleeping bag under the seat.

"Stay," he mouthed at me. I watched from under the bench as his feet retreated.

You can't fight them, Trent! I wanted to shout at him. *They'll kick your tail and throw you over the side!*

But seconds later he was shoving a life jacket at me. I wriggled into it and fumbled with the buckles.

"Now!" he said into my ear.

Then he cupped his hand around my arm and pulled me up onto the seat again. His life jacket was dangling in his other hand.

"Put that on!" I said.

"I will! Jump!"

I was never sure whether I actually jumped or Trent pushed me. I only knew that as my feet left the boat, there was a yell from behind him, and Ethan lunged out of the shadows for Trent's back. I hit the surface on my side, crying out in pain. The life jacket came off and was swept out of my reach. Water rushed down my throat and I came up choking.

I wanted to scream for Trent, but all I could do was cough. I took in more water as I bobbed below the surface, but I could only paddle with one arm and leg to try to keep myself afloat. The other side, I was sure, had been ripped off from the top of my cheek to my knee. Beyond, the roar of the motor receded into the night.

Where was Trent? Panic seized me, and all I could see in my own darkness was Ethan pounding him into the bottom of the boat—or his body, beaten by the propellers, dropping down into whatever this was we were in—

God! God—help! Please—

There was a sound—but it wasn't God. It was the motor, growling toward me again.

But it was coming from the wrong direction. And it didn't shoot straight for me. Lights veered off to the side, and as I squinted into them, I saw a female silhouette.

Don't let it be Gigi, I prayed. But I waved my good arm above my head until I started to sink again. Even she wouldn't let somebody drown, would she?

"Duffy! Duffy—we're throwin' you a line!"

It wasn't Gigi. It was an angel. And her name was Celeste.

Her body was halfway out of a boat much smaller than the one I'd been in, so the whole craft dipped dangerously toward me. Somebody else stood up on the bow and tossed something at me. A ring landed with a splash next to my head.

"Grab onto it, Duffy!" Celeste was shouting. "We'll pull you in!"

I hooked my good arm over it, but I was shaking my head. I could barely open my mouth, and my voice came out muffled and tangled.

"You have to find Trent! He might have gotten knocked out!"

"What's she talking about?"

"Duffy—just hang on—we're bringing you in!"

I clung to the life preserver, but I strained my neck up to search the water as they pulled me through it.

"Trent!" I tried to shout. "Trent—where are you?"

"Duffy—what the—"

"There's a ladder there. Put your foot on it and we'll pull you up."

"We've gotta find Trent—"

"One—two—three—"

Two pairs of hands hauled me into the boat. One of them stayed on me, pulling me into her heaving little chest. "Duffy, thank God," Celeste said. "Just—thank God."

"Did they hurt you?"

I pried myself away from Celeste. Stevie was on her knees beside us.

"Dear—God!" Celeste's eyes registered horror as she stared at my face. "We've got to get her to a hospital!"

Stevie nodded and started to get to her feet, but I snatched at her wrist.

"Listen to me!" I said. Every word was like an ice pick in my ear. "Trent—is—out—here!"

"What are you sayin', Duffy?"

I tried to talk without moving my face. "He got me over the side but Ethan caught him—and I don't know if he made it off the boat."

Stevie looked stricken.

"What?" I said. "What?"

"Let's just hope he did. Those guys are insane."

"So what do we do?" Celeste said. "Do we go after the boat— look for Trent here—Duffy, what?"

They were both looking at me. The boat was starting to spin— they were starting to spin—but they were looking at me as if I knew where the solid ground was. I shook my head and tried not to throw up.

"Okay—look—" Celeste said. She spread out both hands, fingers shaking. "We can't do both. If Trent's out here, we gotta look for him."

"No," Stevie said.

Celeste turned on her like a wet cat. "Enough with the coverin' for your friends—this is *our* friend—"

"I know—and we're not gonna find him by ourselves in the dark." Stevie stood up and grabbed onto the back of the driver's seat. "I'm calling the Coast Guard. There's some ice in that little fridge back there. You oughta get some on Laura's face."

She hiked up onto the back of the seat and pulled a cell phone out of her shoulder bag. Celeste stared at me.

"Who'd a thought?" she muttered to me. "I'm getting you some ice."

But I couldn't just sit there and hold a bag of ice on my face while Trent could be washing up on the shore someplace—although there wasn't much else I *could* do. The two of them set out the anchor because Stevie was afraid she'd run over Trent if she moved any more, and then they edged along the side of the boat, shining flashlights into the water. Every time I tried to move even a little bit, I couldn't breathe for the pain in my side or the pain in my face or the pain in my shoulder. They made me lie down on a padded bench, and I prayed until the Coast Guard's lights flashed across our stern.

"You say you've got somebody hurt on board?" a man shouted to us.

"Yes!"

"No! I'm fine—I want to stay 'til we find him!"

No one listened to me. Two more boats arrived and someone carried me on board one of them and asked me a string of questions about Vance and Ethan and the boat we'd been on. I heard one of the other boats leave us, while mine made a wide swing and purred back across the water.

"Where are we?" I said.

The officer who'd carried me on board got close to me, as if he were having a hard time understanding what I was saying.

"We're in Massalina Inlet. And lucky for you." He pulled a blanket up around my neck and tucked it into the ice bag he'd put along the side of my face. "If you'd ended up out in the Bay, there's no telling when they would have found you."

I could feel tears sliding out of the corners of my eyes and into the hair that was plastered to the sides of my face.

"Soon as we get you to shore, we'll call your parents," he said. "I don't think you need to be talkin' anymore right now."

"Let me just say this one more thing," I whispered to him. "I want somebody to tell me the minute they find Trent—the *minute*."

"Okay, honey. Let's get you taken care of first. I'm going to give you a little oxygen."

Although it did hurt to breathe, I was pretty sure the oxygen was just to shut me up. I heard him murmur, "Whatever happened to just worrying about getting a prom date?"

"Please, God," I whispered.

I felt for the rope. It was there, slack in my soul-hands.

I know. Stay. But please pull Trent out. Please.

An ambulance screamed me to the hospital, where the people in the E.R. wouldn't let Dad in until they'd poked me and prodded me and asked me the same questions ten times. When I told them I'd blacked out right after Vance punched me, there was another string of questions. I didn't get to see Dad until they were rolling me down the hall for X-rays and a C.T. Scan. Even then I only had time to ask him to please find out about Trent before the elevator doors closed him out and they whisked me off to take pictures of every part of my anatomy. When they got me back to the E.R., Mom was allowed to come in and wait with me until the results came in.

"Mom—what's going on?" I said.

"They said not to let you talk—"

"Then *you* talk. Please tell me—"

Mom was barely holding back tears as she told me that Celeste was in the waiting room—the Coast Guard had made her and Stevie come in—and that there was still no word on Trent.

"I don't know how any of this happened," she said, "but I promise you one thing, Laura." She was crying for real now. "If I have to sit on your father, I am going to make him listen to you."

A doctor finally brought Dad in and told us I had a concussion, two cracked ribs, a dislocated shoulder, and a broken jaw.

Nothing they could do about the ribs. They'd probably get my shoulder back into place while I was having surgery to repair my jaw.

"Surgery?" Mom and Dad said in perfect unison.

"Whoever hit her got her pretty hard. She's going to have to be wired shut for a while, I suspect. I hope you're planning to press charges."

"You got that right," Dad said.

It wasn't long before they had me laid out, hooked up, and headed for the operating room, with Mom and Dad trotting along beside me as far as the elevator.

"Before you go to sleep," Dad said, "Celeste made me promise to tell you this."

Suddenly I didn't want to "go to sleep." *What if I didn't wake up? What if I did wake up and they told me they hadn't found Trent? God— what if—*

"Hey—Baby Girl." Dad looked as if he wanted to put his arms around me, only we were moving too fast. "It's going to be fine. They do this all the time. Only not to you, huh? Not to my daughter." He smiled wryly. "There's no doubt in anybody's mind now about whether or not these characters took your car. Looks like there's nothing they won't stoop to." Dad licked his dry lips. "But

Celeste says to tell you you're not the only one ready to take them down. I guess one of their own was reading some of them the riot act when she got to the theatre to look for you."

"Stevie," I said. My jaw was moving a little too easily. So was the room.

"Something like that. She and Celeste got it out of them what was 'going down'—"

I knew in a foggy kind of way that those were Celeste's words.

"—and they took off looking for you—"

Dad seemed to be evaporating like Humpty Dumpty, and I strained to piece him back together. I thought he said they saw my car floating in the water with a guy in a ponytail at the wheel, but I knew I was dreaming.

And then there were no dreams.

* * * * * *

It was a long time, and then again—no time, before I was lying in a hospital bed, riding the waves of pain and morphine. It had to be almost morning by then, but the lights were glaring and there was a steady stream of people flowing around me. Some of them were in green, some of them weren't.

"You need to go home, Celeste," I heard Mom say.

"You promised I could tell her."

"I don't think she's going to remember it." That was Dad. All the king's soldiers and all the king's men must have put him back together again, I thought.

"She'll remember this—"

"Okay—"

"Duffy—"

"Mmmm?" was all I could say. My mouth wouldn't move at all. My teeth seemed to be stuck together.

"—found Trent—ON Their boat—and he's okay!"

I gurgled down in my throat.

"He took 'em both down—locked them in the cabin—doesn't know from motors—just turned it off—threw out the anchor—radioed the cops—"

I opened my eyes and saw her, bedraggled and wet and beautiful, beside my pillow.

No stinkin' way! I said with my eyes.

She grinned. "Way," she said. "Trent rocks."

And then a smooth and silken rope tugged gently at my

mind, and I drifted away.

* * * * * *

They let me go home the next afternoon. After the exhilaration of knowing that Trent was alive and well—things started to crash.

My right arm was in a sling. My side hurt every time I breathed, much less moved.

And my jaw was wired shut so I couldn't talk. I had to eat everything in liquid form, drawn through a giant plastic syringe with a long rubber tube stuck to it. Even though Mom said she could put absolutely anything I wanted through a food processor and a blender, nothing sounded that good to me.

Besides the fact that I was in pain, it finally hit me that I wasn't going to be in *Grease*. Even if I had been able to open my mouth to sing, no amount of make-up could cover the angry black and purple bruise that extended from my swollen-shut eye down to my neck. Some of it was due to the surgery itself, but most of it was Vance Woodruff's handiwork.

That, of course, meant that Detective Lee spent an hour at our house Monday afternoon, asking me questions and trying to sort everything out. Dad took off work to be there

Detective Lee told us everything she knew and what we needed to know to proceed legally. She said Vance and Ethan would be charged with assault, kidnapping, and reckless endangerment. They had already been charged with grand theft auto.

"When we finally got our hands on your vehicle, which was parked down at the marina," she said, "it had their fingerprints all over it. And your friend Stephanie gave us a statement. When she called us before, she'd heard about their plan but since it was her word against theirs, she hadn't thought there was much point in giving her name." The detective gave me a thumbs-up. "She said you inspired her to come forward. I told you you could turn this thing around."

I didn't remember her saying that to me that day at the police station, but I was pretty powerless to argue with her. I was definitely going to have to get a dry-erase board to carry around with me so I could communicate.

"How did you get a hold of the car?" Dad said.

"That's interesting," she said. "Laura's friend Trent said he was waiting for her at the school Sunday evening—to keep an eye on you, Laura. He seemed to have a premonition that this group was going to mess with you, although I'm not sure he knew how far they were willing to go. He didn't expect them to take off with you in a vehicle, and he didn't have wheels, so when the two boys threw you in the truck and drove away, he went after you on foot."

"My word!" Mom said.

"He says he was running down Magnolia Avenue when a young man pulled over in *your* car and said he knew where they were taking you and for Trent to jump in. He said he'd never seen the fella before, although the guy seemed to know him."

I held my breath, and I would have closed my eyes except I wanted to bore them directly into Detective Lee until she had to look at me.

"I guess I owe you an apology, Laura," she said. "Trent said the guy had a ponytail."

I could feel my parents looking at each other above my head in total bewilderment. I snapped my fingers at the pen Detective Lee had behind her ear. She handed me that and a pad of paper. I scribbled furiously on it with my left hand, with Mom and Dad hovering over my shoulder. I wasn't sure which would be harder for any of them to understand, my handwriting or my clenched-teeth talking.

Detective Lee took the pad and read it, lips moving.

"Let me tell you what I think you're saying," she said.

"Mmmm."

"You heard our two little perps discussing on board that they'd originally intended to steal the car and make it look like you'd taken it yourself so you could pin it on them."

"Mmmmmm."

"But then somebody stole it from them."

"Mmmmmmmmmm!"

"Unbelievable," Dad said.

But Detective Lee shook her head. "No more so than THAT thief showing up with the car to get Trent down to the dock at Massalina Marina just in time to hear Laura screaming. Trent jumped on board as the boat was pulling away and hid until he could get Laura alone." She gave a soft grunt. "He says he was 'too much of a wimp' to take them on—which is completely untrue because he ended up doing just that once he got you off of there."

So I hadn't dreamed Celeste's explanation after all.

"What happened to this young man?" Mom said. "I'd like to do something nice for him AND Trent."

"He's a thief, hon," Dad said.

"We'd like to know where he is, too, Mrs. Duffy. Unfortunately, we can neither arrest him nor reward him because once Trent made his dive for the boat, he says he never saw him again. And the car was left at the marina."

I didn't like the way she said it. I might not have been able to speak, but I could narrow my eyes, and she seemed to see the suspicion in them.

"Listen, Laura, I know Trent saved you from even worse injury— "

"Or death," Dad put in.

"But we have to follow up on the possibility that Trent had your car to begin with. That there was no young man with a ponytail."

"NNNNNNN!" I said.

Mom put her hand on the good side of my face, and Dad stepped out from behind the couch.

"She's getting too upset," Dad said.

"I'm sorry. I'll cut this short."

But I was already snatching up the pen and the pad and scribbling—TRENT DOES NOT DRIVE!

Detective Lee shook her head. "He might not have a license, but every teenage boy knows how to drive—"

"Were his fingerprints on the steering wheel?" Dad said.

"Well—no. And I will admit, there were NO other prints except Ethan's and Vance's. Hence my suspicion that there could be no other driver."

"He could have wiped the prints off," Dad said.

"So could Mr. X."

"Then why were the other two kids' prints still there?"

I looked up at Dad with surprised pride. He was asking all the same questions I wanted to ask but couldn't—and he was probably doing a much better job.

Detective Lee looked at me. "The only way I can make a case for this Mr. X. is if your other friend will come forward. The one you said saw this guy with your car in the middle of the night. Her statement and Trent's would give us two witnesses."

I closed my eyes. Why couldn't they just let that part of it die? Vance and Ethan were going to get what was coming to them. If Ponytail Boy had anything to do with it, it was obvious it had been for a good reason.

But then there was Trent. If K.J. didn't corroborate his story, the police might hound him to death. He didn't deserve that.

Slowly I pulled the pad back to me and wrote: I'LL TALK TO HER AGAIN.

"Fair enough," the detective said.

"She's tired now," Dad said. "I want her to get some rest."

"I understand. I'll type up your statement and call you when it's ready to be signed."

She stood up to go, with Dad marching her to the doorway, when she turned back to me.

"Just one more thing you'll want to know, I think. The three girls—Wendy Lewis, Virginia Palmer, and Natalie McNair—have been charged as accessories to kidnapping and auto theft. And while I had them at the station, I was able to charge them with shoplifting as well."

I could feel my eyes bulging.

"Your old boss—" She consulted her clipboard. "Yolanda —well, the woman at The Gap—made the charge, corroborating what you told us. Seems someone came forward as an eyewitness. One of her other employees."

"Hhhhh?" I said.

"He asked that his name not be given out except to us. See—you started an epidemic of integrity, Laura. I'm sorry you had to go through all this, but you've done a good thing."

At the moment I didn't feel like I'd done anything but make trouble for Trent.

When Detective Lee was gone, Dad crouched down beside me. "Who is this girl who needs to vouch for Trent?" he said. "I want to get her over here so you can talk to her."

I pointed, incredulously, to my mouth.

"We can help you—or you can write things down—we'll figure something out."

I gave him a doubtful look.

"Everybody is trying to do the right thing," Dad said. "It looks like you bring that out in people, so why don't you try to bring it out in her?"

"You told that detective you would try," Mom said. "And I'd love to see you prove her wrong. I'm not sure I liked her attitude." Dad and I both stared at her, and then we laughed. It hurt my whole body, but somehow it felt so good.

chapter twenty

A bout ten minutes after school let out that day, our doorbell started ringing. Celeste, of course, was the first one there, and she "babysat" me while Mom went to get Bonnie from school and Dad went to the police impound station to claim my car.

"Did you tell him to take it straight to the junkyard?" she said.

"Mmmmm."

"Okay—so before Mama Duffy gets back with little Jabber Jaws, let me tell you MY part of the story."

"Mmmmmmm!"

"Okay—so Sunday I finally get Joy Beth on the phone and make her talk to me. She finally tells me she's been trying to swim again only she can't because her diabetes is all screwed up and she's just figuring she'll drop out of everything. So I just start going on to Joy Beth about how I didn't actually think there was a God either until I started hanging out with you and how watching you and doing the kinds of things you're doing, you know, like praying and stuff, has already helped me and if she'd just give it a chance she could see there's a lot more to life than swimming—and that we could, like, throw her a rope to keep her going, or whatever that was you told me. Weird, huh, since that's what I ended up doing for you later that night, like, for real. Anyway, I'm saying all this stuff to her, and I'm bawlin' so hard I can't even see, and all of a sudden she just hangs up." Celeste threw her head back and her arms up in the air. "So then I'm like really freakin' out so I go tearing up to the school to try to talk to you before you start—" She took a breath and suddenly grinned at me. "This is pretty weird talking to you when you can't talk back.

"SO—I get to the school and go charging into the theatre, backstage—which I was lucky to get into because it's like Fort Knox back there when there's a rehearsal going on—"

I slumped back into the couch and listened, trying to let the information go inside my brain without getting to my heart, which was already cracked and ready to break. This side of it was worse than all my ailing body parts put together.

She told me K.J. found her ramming around in the Green Room and she was as worked up as Celeste. K.J. told Celeste that Deidre told *her* I hadn't signed in yet, but that Gregor didn't know I was missing so far and neither did Mr. Howitch. K.J. was trying to find me so I wouldn't get in trouble. They both agreed that I wouldn't miss a tech rehearsal unless—well, it just wouldn't happen.

They split up, Celeste told me, and she went through the theatre house and out into the lobby. Stevie was there, backing Gigi and Natalie up against the wall, yelling at them both. Stevie got out of them what Celeste started to figure out the minute she spotted Natalie there, in full stage make-up. Gigi admitted that Vance and Ethan were going to make me "unavailable" until the rehearsal was over, and there would be no way I could escape from them before Natalie had already stepped in to save the day—because they were taking me out in Vance's father's boat.

Stevie took off for the doors, and Celeste followed her. Stevie didn't protest when Celeste jumped in her car with her and they screamed off for the marina. On the way, Stevie told Celeste that Wendy had called her, all hysterical, because They had cut her out of the loop.

"Stevie feels, you know, like a coward for not doing something sooner that could have stopped everything," Celeste said. "But she didn't know it was going to go this far. She'd already started hanging out with Justin all the time, and she thought she could stay out of it."

I nodded.

"She must have one of those rope things going on, too," Celeste said.

I raised my eyebrows.

"Seriously. The whole time me and her were trolling around out there in her dad's boat—that was his SMALL boat—give me a break—anyway, she kept saying, 'Dear Jesus, please let us find her.'" Celeste's blue eyes widened. "And she wasn't swearing, either, Duffy. It was like she was actually praying."

"Mmm," I said.

"Well, you'll believe it when she comes over here tonight."

"Mmmmmm?"

"Yeah. She asked me at school today if I thought it would be okay. We had lunch—me and her and Trent."

I felt the clouds go across my mind.

"What?" she said.

I picked up my pad and wrote, "I have to talk to K.J."

"I'm on it," she said.

She went for the phone, and then Mom came back with Bonnie, who had to examine me with her toy doctor kit and wanted to heal all with boo-boo kisses. Mom told her she had to just blow kisses, for which I was grateful.

They went to the kitchen to make smoothies, and the doorbell rang again. Celeste came in, eyes aglow, with Owen on her heels.

"Look who's here," she said. She wiggled her eyebrows and then disappeared into the kitchen, saying she had to help my mom. As if she'd ever made a smoothie in her life.

Owen just stood there looking at me. I had to remind myself that this was his first glimpse of my Vance Woodruff Makeover. I gave him a minute to force his face out of horror mode and patted the couch next to me.

He sat down gingerly and cocked his head. He was like a puppy, and I wanted to cuddle him. I motioned for the pad and wrote, YOU TURNED IN THEIR ROYAL HIGHNESSES!

When he'd read it, he flipped to the next blank page and doodled while he talked.

"Yeah, I went to Yolanda and told her about the times I caught Wendy and them red-handed. I never told you because I knew you'd think I was a loser for just turning my head."

"Nnnnnnn!"

"Hey, I was. But after we had that talk, you and me, I didn't want to be a loser in your eyes anymore. Plus—I was sick of being one in my own eyes."

"WHAT ABOUT YOUR DAD?" I wrote on the pad.

Owen frowned at it. "I don't remember your handwriting being this bad. Oh, you have to use your left hand. Sorry." He gave me another long look. "Girl, you are all kinds of messed up. I'd like to get my hands on those—guys."

He continued to sketch on the pad. "I called my old man and told him the truth, that I was working at the mall, and just like I knew he would, he said he wouldn't pay anymore of my college expenses."

"Mmmm?"

Owen ran his hand over his hair. It was still that soft brown color. "Man, I lost it. I told him I was working to support Mom because she's so messed up after living with him all those years, she can hardly get out of bed some mornings."

I tilted my head at him.

"He hung up on me. But—get this—my mother—my I'm-nothing, I-can't-cope-with–anything, depressed little mother—called him back and let him have it for being such a jerk to me." Owen shrugged. "It didn't do any good in terms of me getting money from him. But I told her I was proud of her for finally standing up to him, and for the last three days she's been getting up and going to work. I don't know how long it'll last—but I have to tell you something, Laura." He put the pad aside and swiveled to face me, "I'm really glad you can't interrupt me because I have to say this, like, all at once, or I'll wimp out." He took a breath and paused. "I don't know what it is about you, but you make me want to be the person I know I can be. And besides that—"

There was a tap on the doorframe, and Owen jumped off the couch like he'd been hit with a BB gun. I saw the gleam in Mr. Howitch's eyes as he walked into the room.

"Julian Howitch," he said. He stuck his hand out to Owen. "Sorry to interrupt—but can I get an audience with the patient?"

Owen and I looked at each other. Owen was a little green in the face.

"Yes, sir, you go ahead," he said. "I'll call you, Laura—no, that would be pointless, wouldn't it? I'll come back tomorrow—that okay?"

I nodded as hard as I could without hurting my face.

Please get it, I tried to say with my eyes. I WANT you to come back!

He nodded at Mr. Howitch and hightailed it out of there.

Mr. Howitch .sat down and told me how sorry he—and the whole cast— was that I wasn't able to be in the musical. He presented a huge card with everybody's signatures on it.

"When K.J. O'Toole told Gregor and me that you hadn't shown up Sunday night, she practically made me sign a sworn statement that I didn't believe you'd just blown off the rehearsal. She said she could do your part for the night, and I sure wasn't going to let Natalie do it—even though she sailed on stage before anybody but K.J. and Gregor and myself knew you weren't there." Mr. Howitch gave his head a stern shake. "That girl has a real problem—the whole gang of them does. Anyway, K.J. had your part down cold, and she doesn't have a half-bad voice." He leaned over to put a hand on my arm. "She doesn't even begin to come close to you, of course, but she pulls it off. I'm going to go ahead and let her do the part for the run of the show—"

I felt myself go cold. Now K.J. would never tell the police her story. As much as the theatre meant to her, there was no way she was going to jeopardize this chance.

"I'm so sorry, Laura," Mr. Howitch was saying. "But you know this doesn't do anything to change my plans for you for next year. I'm thinking of doing a summer program, so let's talk about that when you feel better."

I nodded and tried not to wilt into the couch. Instead, I focused my energy on trying to look sorry that he had to go. I really needed to be alone.

But he'd no sooner left the room when Mom brought in three smoothies—one for me, one for Celeste, and one for K.J.

I closed my eyes. The silky rope was still there, lying curled in a satin pile. That meant I was supposed to stay. Like I had any other choice.

"Hey, Laura D.," K.J. said, "you look terrible." Celeste poked her. "Of course she looks terrible. You would, too, if you'd been punched out and shoved around and thrown off a boat."

K.J. sat down on the coffee table and folded her legs up Indian style.

"Make yourself comfortable," Celeste said.

"Thanks." K.J. picked up my food-syringe and examined it. "I'm afraid to ask what this is for."

Celeste took it from her. "Could we get to the point before somebody else comes over?"

I put up my hand to get Celeste's attention and then picked up my pad to start writing.

But there was a drawing on the top page—it was unmistakably me with a heart-shaped bruise on my face. Owen had written underneath: MY girlfriend?

As much as it hurt to do it, I smiled, and for a second nothing else mattered.

"What's the deal?" Celeste said.

I shook my head, carefully tore off that page, and pushed it under my afghan.

"Censored," K.J. said.

WE HAVE TO TALK ABOUT PONYTAIL BOY, I wrote on the pad. When I held it up for her, she pulled her legs in tighter.

"Do I have to write back?" she said to Celeste. "Or can I just talk?"

"Well, du-uh—she's the only one who can't speak." Celeste gave me a look that clearly said, *Please deal with this chick—she's driving me nuts!*

I tried to nod reassuringly at K.J. I couldn't antagonize her—for Trent's sake.

GLAD YOU GOT MY ROLE, I wrote.

For the first time since I'd known her, K.J. looked fourteen and vulnerable, instead of twenty-five and ready to do battle at the drop of a word.

"I didn't want it that way," she said.

"She knows that," Celeste said. And she's not mad at you for stepping in. She knows you're a good actor and she doesn't think you were going, 'Yeah— here's my chance!'" Celeste looked at me. "Right?"

K.J.'s head was bobbing, her earrings bouncing against her neck.

"Rrrrrrt," I said.

"You're not supposed to talk, Duffy," Celeste said.

I grabbed the pad and pen and scribbled furiously, showing what I'd written to K.J. at intervals.

I KNOW IF YOUR DAD FINDS OUT ABOUT—YOU KNOW— K.J. went stiff.

BUT WITHOUT ANOTHER WITNESS TO THE GUY WITH THE PONYTAIL HAVING MY CAR, THEY THINK TRENT STOLE IT FROM VANCE—

K.J. looked away from the pad, from me, from everything as she stared up at the ceiling. Celeste started to say something, but I nudged her with my foot. I could almost hear the wheels turning in K.J.'s head, and that was a better sound than an out-and-out "no way."

Throw her a rope.

It was another sound—a whisper—and it startled me. It hadn't said *stay*. But *Throw her a rope*? How was I supposed to tell her about God while scribbling on a pad of paper?

Celeste.

I closed my eyes. It was hard to tell whether that was the Voice, or just me, or me already knowing what God wanted me to do. It was a little scary.

"You okay?" Celeste said. "You want I should get Mama Duffy?"

I shook my head and grabbed for the pen.

TELL K.J. ABOUT THE ROPE, I wrote.

When I held it up to Celeste, her eyes widened. I could clearly read the expression on her face as she pulled her head forward at me like E.T.: *You want me to talk to HER, about God? Did that concussion leave you wacko?*

I nodded at her. *You can do it,* I told her with my eyes. And then I wrote, FOR TRENT.

Celeste whipped her face immediately toward K.J., who was watching us.

"Okay, look," Celeste said to her. "I'm gonna tell you what Laura would tell you if she could talk. It's gonna sound weird, but I know it's totally the truth because I've seen it happen."

K. J. gave an exaggerated shrug. "Okay," she said, "knock yourself out." She folded her arms across her chest.

"Okay, so here's the way it is," Celeste said. "Laura believes in God. A lot of people say they do, but she REALLY does. And she spends all this time praying and reading the Bible and writing in her journal and talking to Mrs. I., so it's like. , she's gotten to where she gets these feelings and she knows it's God. Sometimes it's like a whisper, and sometimes it's a—what do you call it—like a symbol or something. Like lately, it's been like this rope made of silk and it either pulls her to do something, or it just sits there, which means she's supposed to wait it out. Are you getting all this, O'Toole?"

"Yeah—"

"Okay, so that whole rope thing is why she told the cops about Vance and them—and why she turned Wendy and those other chicks in for shoplifting. And whenever she's supposed to help somebody, it'll be like she's supposed to throw the rope—you know, figuratively speaking—to them. So now—" Celeste took a just-before-passing-out breath "So now, we gotta throw the rope to you."

K.J. looked at me as if I'd been the one talking the whole time. "What's that got to do with me blowing the whistle on Ponytail Boy?"

I nodded my head toward Celeste.

"What?" she said. "Like I know!"

"Yyyyyy dddddddddd," I said.

Celeste bulged her eyes at me. "I'm about to clip those wires."

But I just nodded. That was the feeling I was getting—to let her take K.J. where we needed her to go.

"Well, somebody tell me," K.J. said. "Because so far—"

Celeste put her hand up. "Okay—don't get your panties in a bunch. Here's the deal—I think. Every time Laura's been pulled by this rope thing from God, it's been to do the right thing, tell the truth, and let everything else fall into place."

"Which is why she's sitting here with her arm in a sling and her jaw wired shut, and I'm doing her part in the musical." K.J. narrowed her eyes at Celeste. "That's really falling into place."

I reached up and pulled the pen out of Celeste's hair and scrawled—MIGHT NOT BE PERFECT FOR ME—

"Ya think?" K.J. said. She gave a high-pitched false laugh.

BUT YOU GOT THE PART—I FOUND OUT A BOY THAT I LIKE LIKES ME TOO—BECAUSE OF ALL THIS.

"And Trent doesn't think he's just a big wimp anymore," Celeste said. "And Stevie's finally out of Their group, which is something she's wanted to happen for a long time. What's a little bruise compared to all that?"

K.J. gave me a dubious look. "That's more than a 'little bruise.'" BUT IT'S STILL WORTH IT TO ME. I FEEL GOOD—EXCEPT ABOUT TRENT— "You can stand not being in the musical?" K.J. said. "When singing's, like, your big thing?"

I nodded and wrote: THERE'S ALWAYS NEXT YEAR.

"But not for me! If I get busted for being out of my house at three in the morning, my father will pull me out of the show so fast—and that will be it for Mr. Howitch. This was my last chance. There won't be a next year for me."

Both Celeste and I stared at her because she was on the edge of tears. I could hear them trembling in her voice, see her trying to blink them back from the edges of her lower lids.

TALK TO MR. HOWITCH FIRST, I wrote.

"You can't talk to teachers about stuff like that!"

"Oh, really?"

We all turned to the doorway, where Mrs. I. was standing, hands in the pockets of her denim skirt as if she'd been there for a while.

"I take exception to that, K.J.," she said. "You mind if I join this conversation?"

I nodded, but she was still looking at K.J.

"Whatever," K.J. said. "Just bring the whole world in here to gang up on me."

"If that's the case—" Mrs. I. turned to look over her shoulder and called out, "Come on in, Stevie."

By now K.J. was looking so miserable, I almost called a halt to the whole thing.

Almost.

Celeste made room for Stevie at the end of the couch. I wrote THANK YOU SO MUCH on the pad and showed it to her. Stevie gave me a smile so genuine I felt as if I'd just stepped through a door I hadn't even known I'd wanted to open.

"We'll talk," she whispered to me.

"Now," Mrs. I. said. "What were you saying about not being able to talk to teachers?"

"You're different," K.J. said.

"I'm not that different from Mr. Howitch. He doesn't have a successful program just because he's a great musician. It works because he loves you kids and he wants to help you grow. What I'm seeing here is you struggling to do that very thing." Mrs. I. gave K.J. a soft look. "Darlin', he's not going to turn his back on you now—especially after what he's seen you do these past few days."

"MMMM?" I said.

"I stepped in for you because I knew the part from watching rehearsals," K.J. said.

"And?" Mrs. Isaacsen said.

I cocked my head at K.J.

"I got everybody in the cast and crew to sign a card today," K.J. said.

"And?"

K.J. rolled her eyes. "It was no big deal. There were all these rumors going around about Laura and Vance and Ethan and stuff—and none of it was even close to being true—" She shrugged. "So during lunch hour, I stood up on a table and told everyone what was true and what wasn't. I'm telling you, it was no big deal."

"No big deal?" Stevie said. "You had people heckling you and throwing things and you just shut them right up. They all walked away from there knowing the truth."

Mrs. Isaacsen gave K.J. a nudge. "You did that thing you do so well—you know what you think and you speak out about it." She grinned. "And for once it was for a cause that didn't get you suspended."

"Okay, fine, so I'm this big hero," K.J. said. "But I'm not gonna be a martyr—and if I go to the cops about this guy with the ponytail driving Duffy's car I will be freakin' Joan of Arc, because it'll get straight to my father that I was out in the middle of the night and he will ground me until I'm forty."

"Why would your father know?" Stevie said.

"Because he's the chief of police."

"Does every little case go through him?" Celeste asked.

I picked up the pen and wrote: THE POLICE WILL PROTECT THE IDENTITY OF A WITNESS, IF THEY REQUEST IT. THEY DID IT FOR SOMEBODY ELSE.

Three of them read it out loud in unison, but K.J. still shook her head. "I can't get up on a witness stand with a bag over my head. You have to state your name right in court."

"There's never going to be a trial," Stevie said.

She shook back her hair. "My father's a lawyer—he's already refused to represent Vance and them, by the way—and he told me this won't go beyond a preliminary hearing because there's so much evidence against them." She twisted up her mouth for a second. "And besides, do you really think Mr. Woodruff and Mr. Palmer and the other ritzy parents want this paraded through the courts? My dad says they'll probably plead guilty and get a lesser sentence."

K.J. looked tearful again. "You really think that's going to happen?" she said. "What if it doesn't?"

"That's where God comes in," Celeste said. "I mean, God's there the whole time—but that's where you'll really know there's, like, this lifeline to hang onto."

"I don't see any lifeline," K.J. said.

But her voice was trembly and yearning, and I could feel that maybe she wanted one.

WE CAN HELP YOU, I wrote.

"She definitely can," Celeste said with a nod in my direction.

"Yeah," said another voice. "She can."

That came from a figure lurking in the doorway. I started to cry when I saw it was Joy Beth – and that Trent was pushing her from behind.

"Joy Beth's got something to say," he told us.

Joy Beth looked at us from between two panels of hair. Trent took her hand and they entwined fingers.

Celeste gave me a *Too cute!* look.

"Ever since this happened," Joy Beth said, "it's been like ya'll were pullin' at me or something." She shrugged the big shoulders. "So now I'm back. And it's because of that."

I figured—with a lump in my throat—that Joy Beth had said her entire quota of words for the next three weeks, if not longer.

All eyes were now on K.J., and her face went through emotions like cards flipping past on a Rolodex. Around her, the room was holding its breath, waiting to see where the rolling would stop. When her face crumpled and she finally gave way to the tears she'd been holding back, I knew. Or at least I hoped I knew.

She put her hands over her eyes, pressing against them until I was sure it had to hurt.

"Do you all swear—swear—that you won't tell anybody else about this?" she said.

Hands went up all over the room.

The fingers came away from her eyes, although she didn't look up. "And you won't all bail on me if I get grounded or kicked out of the theatre program—or both?"

"Try to get rid of us," Celeste said. "I'm speaking for me and Duffy—and Joy Beth."

"Count me in," Stevie said.

Trent did some shuffling around, which seemed to be affirmative.

K.J. took in so much air I could see her belly expanding. .

"Okay," she said. "I'll talk to the police—only not at the station. I don't want my father walking in." I went for the pad again and wrote, DETECTIVE LEE WILL COME HERE.

"Now?" K.J. said. "It has to be now or I'm gonna lose my nerve."

"I'm gonna go ask Laura's dad to call that detective," Celeste said. "You better come with, K.J."

Trent looked completely confused as he and Joy Beth followed them out, but I knew Celeste would fill him in—and then some.

"I need to go, too," Stevie said when they'd left. "But could I ask something?"

"Sure," Mrs. I. said.

Stevie suddenly looked shy. "Do you think I could join this group, too? I mean, if it's too full—" Mrs. I. looked at me. I was nodding and begging her with my eyes.

"Absolutely, Stevie," she said. "It means a commitment to

come during your activity period on Tuesdays and Thursdays, and I know you're involved in a lot of things."

"Nothing I want to stay involved in." Stevie looked down at her hands. "I think this is more important than anything I'm doing. I know it is."

Then she reached over and squeezed my hand and hurried out.

I sank back into my pillows and gurgled down in my throat and felt a wobbly relief all over, even in the parts that hurt.

"I'm so proud of you, Laura," Mrs. Isaacsen said.

I shook my head. "Gddddd."

"God? God did it all?"

I nodded. I hoped my good eye was as shiny as it felt.

She smiled back at me, not a wrinkle in sight. "Then I think you've found your second power. The power of discipline."

I knew what she meant now, and I nodded.

"And the key, of course, is—" She reached into the pocket of her skirt and pulled out a fist. When she opened it, palm up, there was a tiny silver key that was a little more ornate than my first one. "Obedience. That silky rope you described to me?"

"Mmmhmmm."

"As long as you followed that, you were obeying God. He never pulled you in the wrong direction, did He?"

"Nnnnn."

"And He never will—especially because you're sharing those secret powers with people who are ready to perceive them." Her eyes glowed at me like two orbs of amber. "Did you see what happened in here tonight?"

I nodded.

"It's only going to get better and better." She held up a finger. "Not easier and easier, mind you."

I grunted.

"You already know that. But it's such a good thing."

"Laura?"

It was Mom whispering from the doorway. She had a baffled look on her face that I wanted to soothe away. I wanted everybody to feel the kind of calm and clarity I was feeling.

"When Stevie was leaving, she found this on the front step," Mom said.

She stepped into the room with a small chest in her hands—a treasure chest.

I sat up straight. It was—the one.

Only it couldn't be. This one was beautifully polished, and

its brass shone with an almost unearthly glow.

"There's a note here," Mom said.

My heart stopped beating. She handed me an off-white parchment envelope with my name in calligraphy on the front.

"Should we be careful?" Mom said. "I mean, with all the shenanigans that have gone on—"

But I shook my head and handed the envelope to Mrs. I. to open. My heart was now beating so fast it made my ribs ache, a somehow delicious pain.

Mrs. I. handed the note to me.

You know where your treasure is now.

No one will ever destroy it or steal it from you. Know

that, too.

Your Secret Admirer

The calm settled over me again. Neither Mom nor Mrs. I. said a word as with one hand I lifted the lid—the lid that no longer had a lock on it. Inside was a white rope—made of silk. I looked at Mrs. Isaacsen, but she sat with her head tilted, her face innocent and curious and genuine. I shut off the list of suspects that started to form in my head, the people who knew about the rope.

"Everything all right?" my mother said.

All I could do was nod. When I could, I would tell her AND my father just how all right everything was.

In fact, I might just share it with everybody.

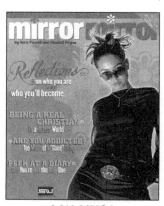